Miranda stepped back, a small cry of despair foaming on her lips. He wanted her and she wanted him and in this heaven here on earth who would know? It was another world, far removed from reality.

He stood in front of her, his breath coarse and rasping, coming from somewhere deep inside him. Miranda let the conch-shell drop to her side, didn't hear the thud of it in the deep sand. All she could hear was its hidden secret, the sea rushing in her ears, roaring wildly.

'Miranda.' He said her name roughly, regrettably, hopelessly.

She murmured what he wanted to hear in the tone he wanted to hear. 'Louis,' she urged softly.

But another screamed out from her. From the part of her that she'd closed off. Catherine, the sea murmured, and as Louis's mouth closed over hers the roaring in Miranda's ears swept it away with a rush of heat and liquid fire.

OFFER ME
A RAINBOW

BY
NATALIE FOX

MILLS & BOON LIMITED
ETON HOUSE   18-24 PARADISE ROAD
RICHMOND   SURREY   TW9 1SR

First published in Great Britain 1992 by Mills & Boon Limited

© Natalie Fox 1992

*Australian copyright 1992
Philippine copyright 1992
This edition 1992*

ISBN 0 263 77470 8

*Set in Times Roman 11 on 12 pt.
01-9203-46742 C*

Made and printed in Great Britain

CHAPTER ONE

MIRANDA aimed the rifle at the head of the stranger swimming smoothly towards her across the bay unaware his life and death were so closely paralleled.

Two days and nights his yacht had been moored beyond the coral reef, and now he was braving that treacherous reef to get to her.

Bare feet apart, her long slender body smooth and taut with bronzed fitness, she stood on a grassy knoll overlooking the white beach. Tensing her naked shoulder into the butt of the rifle, Miranda held his dark head in her sight and then slowly moved the barrel five feet to the left of him, held her breath and squeezed the trigger.

White water sprayed and the crack of the shot sent every parakeet on the tiny Caribbean island of El Paraiso squawking their fury at her for disturbing the balmy tranquillity of the afternoon.

Miranda uttered a curse as the swimmer ploughed on, his powerful body cleaving the water with scarcely a ripple. She aimed again, this time two feet to the left of his head.

'Nerves of steel,' she muttered tightly as he powered on, ignoring the second warning shot that cracked so dangerously close to him.

'See how you like this!' She waited till he came ashore, sent a spray of sugary sand into the air just

inches from his feet as he stood on the beach, raking
sea water from his dark, glistening hair.

The stranger looked down at the disturbance
then, only mildly interested. Slowly he raised his
head and looked up to where the shot had come
from, shielding his dark eyes from the sun.

'Come one step further on to this island and I'll
aim between your eyes!' she screamed down at him.

To her surprise and disdain, he raised his arms
mock defensively, a grin, as wide as the coral reef
he'd so expertly negotiated to get here, spreading
across his face.

Miranda was tempted to chase that grin from his
face with another shot, was tempted even further
when he said, along with that mocking smile,
'Sorry, sweetheart, didn't realise I was trespassing.
I just came ashore to borrow a cup of sugar.'

Anger compressed into fury. Borrow a cup of
sugar? I suppose he thinks that's funny! She spun
round and ran towards the steep path she'd worn
over the last few months, hurtled down to the beach
through thick ferns and scented oleander to tackle
him. See how funny he thinks this is!

The stranger was nowhere in sight. For an instant, fear coupled with fury and knotted painfully
in Miranda's stomach and she tightened her grip on
the rifle. Then too late she whirled. He was upon
her before she could catch her breath to scream. A
huge tanned body, powered by a force that winded
her, wrenched at the rifle.

One hand gripped her upper arm, searing her skin
with the agony of an iron band, flesh on flesh par-

alysing the fears rushing through her head. The other hand flung her uncle's rifle out to sea. It spun in the air as if it were but a feather to this giant of a man who restrained her fury so effortlessly.

Struggling pathetically, Miranda resorted to spitting her fury. 'Let me go, you filth!'

He did, instantly, with a powerful thrust that hurled her backwards. She lost her balance, stumbled and fell back into the sand, her wild raven hair tumbling around her face and shoulders, her thin cotton pareu flying in the breeze exposing her long tanned legs. Her hands flew to the cotton and she covered herself frantically.

'There's no need to be so rough,' she bleated, struggling to her knees and brushing the sand from her arms.

'Typical,' he breathed over her, no smile now to throw her off guard as he raked bitterly, 'You try to blow my head off, separate my toes from my feet and then grizzle when I nearly give you the hiding you deserve.'

He reached down to help her up but Miranda misinterpreted the movement and fearfully scuttled away from him on her knees. She didn't want him touching her again, not ever.

He lurched towards her and hauled her to her feet. 'Don't be so damned dramatic! I'm not going to hurt you . . .'

'Aren't you?' she hurled back, her dark brown eyes narrowing suspiciously. 'I'm easy prey without my gun, aren't I? But I warn you, I'll fight you to the death if you try any funny stuff!'

It was then he threw his head back and laughed, a roar that started the parakeets off again and sent consternation prickling down Miranda's spine. Who was this man and what did he want on her uncle's private island? He'd been anchored out there in the bay for two days and nights, watching her watching him. With the gun she hadn't been afraid; now she felt naked and vulnerable. Naked! She was, under her scarlet pareu! He could whip it away in a split second . . .

He stopped laughing, his jet eyes cold now. 'Have you looked at yourself lately, sweetheart? You're hardly gaol-bait material.'

'You don't look the sort to be too choosy!' she retorted hotly.

She stood firmly on the hot sand facing him. She could imagine what she looked like after three months living rough, and didn't care one bit. These days she only answered to herself. Once she had been at the point of obsession with her appearance. Her fiancé, Presler, had demanded it. Now he was gone and no one was about to step into his shoes and make more demands on her and her life.

The movement of her hand to sweep the long fall of her unkempt hair from her face was instinctive *and* irritating. So maybe the stranger had hit a raw nerve, maybe she had let herself go.

He wasn't so sharp himself! Sun-bronzed like her, his own hair was a turmoil of sea, sand and the ravages of a tropical breeze. He wore faded black Bermuda shorts with a rent down the left thigh exposing tanned muscled flesh which suggested he went as naked as she often did on the islands. He hadn't shaved for days and blue-black growth around his face added a piratical earthiness to his features; nevertheless she recognised a dangerously attractive man when she saw one...

'Who are you and what are you doing on this island? It's private property, you know.' She was calm now. No longer afraid of the stranger who'd hurled the rifle into the sea. If he'd meant to harm her he'd have hung on to it, used it to his own advantage.

'Louis Mendoza,' he said, not offering his hand in the traditional British way. Though his name suggested Portuguese descendency his accent was pure Cambridge.

'Miranda Gordon,' she offered back, surprised at her own politeness considering his lack of it.

'I know who you are,' he said quietly, his black eyes holding hers, gauging her reaction.

Miranda's heart pumped dangerously at that. No wonder he hadn't wanted to shake her hand! After the initial shock of hearing that he knew exactly who she was, her reaction was swift, resolute and to Louis Mendoza probably predictable. She spun in the sand and ran up the track to the grassy knoll and beyond to the wooden shack she had defected to when judgement had been passed on her uncle— a term of imprisonment that would ensure he ended his days under lock and key.

There were no locks or keys to the hut she had lived in these past months; if there were she would have used them to ward off this Mendoza who had trailed up the path after her.

She stood defiantly on the shady wooden veranda, and faced him.

'What exactly is it you want?' she iced, her lips drawn into a tight line of aggression. 'If you think you can offer me millions for my story, no sale.'

'You have nothing to sell,' he told her coolly. 'You hardly know your uncle and even less about his rackets.'

Miranda's stomach somersaulted recklessly. How right he was. She scarcely knew her uncle though he controlled her life. This man knew more about her than was healthy. If he wasn't from the Press, why else was he being so persistent? She stemmed a thread of fear that ran through her. Her uncle had destroyed a lot of people's financial lives; maybe Mendoza was one of them and was out for revenge.

'You seem to know a lot about me,' she said hesitantly, nevertheless tilting her chin bravely.

'Enough,' he drawled.

'Well, I know nothing about you and don't waste your breath enlightening me. Just push off and leave me alone!'

'Sadly, I'm not able to do that,' he murmured as he stepped past her and entered the one-roomed hut.

'Where the hell do you think you're going?' Miranda cried, lunging after him and grabbing at his arm. 'This is private property! Get out of here!'

He pulled his arm away from her clutches and looked around at the basically furnished room. From the two bunks, side by side at one end of the room, to the brightly coloured Mexican rug on the worn wooden floor, to the white painted dressing-table under the window with no glass. The hut on El Paraiso had been used by Miranda's uncle as a stopping-off point on his fishing trips. No one had ever lived there, until Miranda and her dented emotions had taken up residence.

'Where do you cook?' he asked, a question so surprising she answered it.

'Outside—there's a lean-to at the back through that curtain.'

Louis Mendoza crossed the room and parted the green and yellow striped curtain. Outside there was a small porcelain sink mounted on the side of the hut, a bucket under the drainpipe to catch the spillage. Miranda had built a crude stone barbecue beyond the lean-to and that was where she cooked.

'Very primitive,' he uttered, raising Miranda's hackles.

'What else would you expect on a primitive island?' she scathed. 'And what's it to do with you anyway?'

He shrugged his huge shoulders. 'Everything and nothing,' he said mysteriously.

He strode across the back yard to the enclosure she had fenced off with cane and wattle fashioned by herself till her fingers had bled—a small, cultivated plot she had worked and wept over. Tomatoes grew vigorously, fertilised with seaweed she had dived for. A tiny section of herb garden thrived miraculously in the heat. Fennel, dill and rosemary. Bananas and yams and bread-fruit grew beyond the enclosure.

Miranda had survived. A purgatory effort she was only just beginning to feel might have been a success. She no longer felt bitter about Presler; even her uncle's sins had eased from her shoulders. But had this self-imposed exile been in vain now that this man and his arrogance had invaded her privacy?

Miranda watched Louis Mendoza step beyond the enclosure and head towards the fresh-water pool. He knew this island, knew who she was. In that way he intrigued her. On a personal level she didn't like him; arrogance and scorn like his she would have to face if she dared expose herself to the real world once again. She wasn't sure she was ready for that yet. Wearily she went after him.

'Is this where you bathe and take your fresh water from?' he asked when she went and stood beside him on the edge of the deep pool that was fed by a waterfall and filtered by an underground fissure in the rock.

'I don't bathe here,' she admitted, not offering the truth that the pool terrified her. The fissure in the rock had dragged at her legs the only time she had ventured in. It had panicked her, made her realise her vulnerability if an accident occurred in such a place, heightened her awareness that she was alone in the world. No one to rescue her or even care if she lived or died.

She gave herself a mental shakedown. 'I bathe in the sea. I'd be stupid to pollute my own drinking water, wouldn't I?' she huffed, then tossed her wild hair and ran back to the hut.

Minutes later he joined her, in no rush. He moved as the West Indians moved, gracefully, slowly, unhurried in the heat of the tropics. He sat on the cane chair by the table on the veranda as if he'd sat there before. Miranda was sure he had, but not since she had taken up occupancy. Two days ago, narrowing her eyes against the sun, she had caught first sight of him, watching her from the deck of his boat anchored in the bay.

'Can I offer you a drink before you go?' she offered pointedly. 'I have rum and mango juice, but no ice, I'm afraid.'

He smiled then, white against bronze, a devastating combination. Miranda tensed at the thought that threaded through her. She hadn't touched a human being for nearly three months. His assault on the beach had frightened her and, dared she admit it, excited her.

She turned and went inside the hut, her fingers trembling as she wiped two glasses before shakily pouring two measures of rum and topping it up with thick mango juice she had squeezed herself. It was hardly a thirst-quenching drink— more a heady panacea for troubled, restless minds. She'd needed it less and less lately. She needed it now, though; Louis Mendoza disturbed her in more ways than one.

'How do you get your supplies?' he asked when she set the drink down in front of him.

Miranda sat on the veranda steps, her back towards him, her raven hair cascading beyond where her pareu knotted halfway down her back. 'Varga, the fisherman, brought me out from St Vincent. He calls every few weeks to see if there is anything I want.' She sipped her drink. 'I don't need a lot. I've managed to exist well on what the island offers.'

He laughed softly behind her. 'I don't know whether to admire you or have you certified when I get you back...'

She swivelled on the wooden veranda to look at him, her dark eyes wide. 'What do you mean, when you get me back?'

'You can't hide here forever. There's a life out there waiting to be lived.'

'Very profound,' she huffed, 'but that doesn't apply to me; and who are you to tell me what to do?'

'Nobody,' he murmured, offering her nothing more.

She turned back to gazing out over the knoll to the deep turquoise of the Caribbean sea where it merged into the dark blue of the sky. 'You've told me only your name; you know who I am, so I presume you know who my uncle is. You still haven't told me what you want of me.'

'I don't want anything of you—just to escort you back to civilisation. I think you've had long enough to mourn over what might or might not have been.'

With a frown Miranda stood up and went and sat at the cane chair across from him. She wondered what this man knew about her and her life and why he thought he should take it on himself to interfere in her future.

'I'm over twenty-one and entitled to do what I please,' she told him somewhat churlishly. 'I don't want to go back—not yet.' She lowered her dark lashes, picked at a fold of her pareu. She wasn't ready. The time would come when she would have to return; but to where and with whom? There were decisions she hadn't been prepared to make.

'You can't stay here any longer. You'll go mad...'

'So I'll go mad!' Miranda snapped back. 'What does it matter and who cares anyway?' She gulped furiously at her drink. As she lowered it to the rickety table it was plucked from her fingers and hurled into the lush undergrowth.

'Grow up, will you?' Louis Mendoza grated as she stared at him stupefied. 'Guns and drink are lethal in the hands of the inexperienced and not very feminine either.' His eyes narrowed threateningly. 'And don't give me that little-girl-lost treatment. You're not stupid. Stay here any longer and it will be even worse when you do come out and face the world. Another thing: don't overestimate your importance. You might be Sagan Gordon's niece, but he kept you well under wraps. Educated you the other side of the world. You barely know him and there aren't many people who know of your existence, so don't try and give the impression of nursing some sort of damaged pride...'

'Just a minute, you damned interfering, sancti-monious, pushy creep!' Miranda's eyes were black with rage. 'I don't know who you are and I'm not interested, but don't you come here and start preaching to me. I know exactly who I am and I've never credited myself with a smidgeon of impor-tance. I'm not afraid of the world out there; I just need a period of adjustment. Little girl lost,' she mimicked, standing up to stress her point, her palms flat on the table. 'Too damned right I am...'

Louis Mendoza's eyes narrowed at her outburst, his fingers tightened round the glass of punch he had barely touched.

'I've been educated in the best schools,' Miranda went on forcefully. 'I've had everything money can buy; but how do you think I felt when I found that my life had been bought with black money? My uncle was a criminal, amassed a fortune through cheating innocent people. I didn't know that...'

'It took you one helluva long time to find out...'

'Are you implying that I knew all along? Let me tell you I didn't! The first I knew was when my uncle was arrested.'

'And the first hint of trouble and you took off like a rat from a sinking ship.' His voice dripped contempt and Miranda blazed inside.

'No, I did not! I went through every agonising day of that trial,' she blurted heatedly. 'They tore my uncle apart. Supposed Mafia connections, laundering money, every fraudulent dealing you could imagine. It was all news to me. Twenty-two, my life paid for with money embezzled from innocent people.' Her dark brown eyes appealed to him. 'How do you think I felt? I'll tell you—hurt and bewildered and shocked. The repercussions on my life were catastrophic. I was engaged to a New York lawyer who dropped me like a hot potato when a guilty verdict was pronounced at the trial. Not when my uncle was arrested. Oh, no, Presler was sharp enough to realise he might have got off, then I would have been a good catch—the only heir of a very wealthy man. But suddenly I'm penniless and my uncle is in prison and Presler walked out on me.'

She let him absorb that before finalising tightly, 'I've reason to be the way I am, Louis Mendoza! So don't try and interfere in my life; just get off this island and leave me in peace.'

He said nothing, didn't even glance at her. His hand came up to rake through his now dry hair, then he leaned his forearms on his thighs and stared down at the warped boards of the veranda.

So she had finally got through to him, bared her soul in the process; but so what? She'd never see him again. She didn't even want to know what had spurred him to come here in the first place, or how well he knew her uncle. She wasn't even curious to know if he was a criminal too.

She tightened the scarlet cotton round her and walked away from the hut, hoping by the time she returned he would be gone. It was nearly time for the sunset, a calming ritual she witnessed every night from an outcrop of rocks on the small beach. For the third night his yacht was anchored in the bay, and added to the beauty of the sight. The crimson, flaming sun dropping so swiftly behind it, silhouetting the sleek lines of its bow and stern against the burnt-orange sky.

Darkness fell quickly in the Caribbean and Miranda held no fear of the hot dark nights. The island was tiny and far from the nearest civilisation and Louis Mendoza, her first unwelcome visitor. She would be glad when he up-anchored and got on his way to wherever.

'What are you doing?' she asked when she returned to the hut, dismayed to find him still there and, worse, swirling a pan of greenish slime over the fire outside. He'd found her precious few candles and lit them to work by.

'Making callalou soup. It grows wild here. I didn't think I'd be able to persuade you off this island tonight so I'm cooking supper.' He said it so coolly and calmly that Miranda was almost struck speechless—almost but not quite.

'I thought I'd made it clear to you, I'm not leaving my uncle's island!'

'My island,' he corrected levelly.

Miranda was struck speechless then but her body reacted violently to the shock. She shot forward and snatched the pan from his grasp. Like lightning he whipped it back from her and slammed it down on the barbecue grill. His eyes glittered angrily in the candlelight.

'So now you know,' he told her curtly. 'You're trespassing on *my* property.' He turned back to the pan and stirred it slowly.

How could he deliver such a statement and calmly go on stirring that sludge? Miranda wanted to slop it out into the undergrowth. Biting her lip, she kept her cool.

'I think you must have confused this island with another,' she told him emphatically. 'This belongs to my uncle, as do three others on this necklace of islands. Four of his possessions that weren't seized when he was arrested. I've been here before, when we cruised the islands. We stopped here; it was my uncle's favourite. That was his hunting rifle you hurled into the sea... Are you listening to me?'

He turned then and faced her. He looked bored, as if this was the last place on earth he wanted to be but he was putting up with it because he was forced too. But he didn't look the sort of man who did anything but exactly what he pleased; so why that look?

'Yes, I'm listening,' he pronounced on a sigh. 'And I also know what's coming—an eruption of questions and demands for proof, no doubt.'

'Wrong! You're a liar and that's that! This is my uncle's island and it's you who is trespassing.' She took a deep breath. 'I want you off here; now isn't soon enough.'

'I'm not leaving without you...'

'And you're not leaving with me!' she fired back hotly. 'I don't want to go yet!'

'You have no choice and I have no choice but to take you off here, by force or otherwise.' He paused to gaze at her inert fury, his mysterious eyes flicking suggestively over her lithe, taut form. Miranda tensed inside. The look was blatantly sexual—she felt it, sensed it, smelt it. And he knew the effect that look had on her. He stepped towards her, his arm snaking round her waist, forcing her body hard against his. His breath when he spoke fanned warm and sensual on her cheek.

'Three months without a man; I could seduce you off this island now if I wanted too.'

He expected her to struggle, put up some sort of feminine, girlish protest, make him feel macho and virile when he crushed her protestations with a searing kiss. Yes, she'd read all the romances. She smiled.

'I dare say you could,' she murmured, adding a false gasp of pleasure as his hand moved up her back. With a small, soft movement she released the knot of her pareu before he reached it, she eased it away from her naked body and with nerves of iron pressed her body against his own near-naked form.

Every muscle of his that came into contact with her warm, scented skin tensed to breaking-point. Miranda smiled to herself. It had worked.

'Not so much fun when it's offered to you on a plate, is it?' she murmured softly, bravado spurring her on to run her fiery lips across his cheek and nibble at his earlobe. She knew his sort, knew the games men like him played. The chase was all. Well, this time there was no chase. Let him believe he could possess her without a struggle and he'd soon cool off!

'What the...?' she cried, her breath trapping the rest of her protestations in her throat.

His mouth swooped down to hers, took her by surprise and parted her full lips before the heat hit her. Her head spun wildly and her insides contracted so sharply and viciously that she felt physical pain in her groin. In a flash all nerve-endings were on alert as the kiss, delivered with such expertise, lengthened and deepened into a parody of love-making. His tongue probed and caressed and hardened till she wanted to scream with frustration. The need to hurt him physically for exposing her need so cruelly powered her molten rage.

'No, you don't!' he grated hotly against her cheek as he trapped her knee between his thighs before it reached its intended target. 'Don't like it when your bluff is called, do you? Dangerous game, Miranda, sweetheart, very dangerous.'

No games now; he held her with such ferocity that she felt sick and afraid inside. She wanted to cover her nakedness, shame now humiliating her and shrinking her in his arms. He eased her away to look at her; she could see the narrowing of his eyes as they raked every curve of her body. He drank it all in, sated his desire with his eyes. She knew then if she gave the slightest encouragement he would take her.

With a small sob she snatched up her pareu from the ground and, trailing it behind her, ran like the wind to the fresh-water pool. Her bare feet, normally so sure on the uneven terrain, skidded and floundered. She fell, got up and pulled the thin cotton round her waist, in the heat of the night leaving her breasts bare. He wouldn't follow; somehow she knew that for sure.

She collapsed by the side of the pool, lay panting and sobbing face down in the thick, spongy moss that grew close to the water. Her naked breasts, her nipples still taut with that aching need he had so easily aroused, pressed into the moss. Not in all the three months of her exile had she felt like this— that sickening ache throbbing through her, the need for a man to love her, caress her, possess her.

Her hands splayed out above her head and her fingers clawed and gripped the moss tightly as she moved her hips against the ground beneath her. She cried then, huge sobs that hurt her chest and throat. Damn him for coming here! She had been coping and now he had ruined everything!

Later Miranda flung herself on to her back and stared up at the stars in the sky. There was a moon now, bright and white, awash in a milky haze. Mendoza was right; she couldn't go on hiding away from the world. She would go back, get a job somewhere. Had she really got to the age of twenty-two without having had to earn her own living? Her uncle had spoiled her. And yet she had coped here on El Paraiso, survived when all the odds were against her. No electricity, water to be hauled from the pool, no sanitation, no coffee for the past four weeks... Yes, she was a survivor, and this island paradise had proved it. Maybe now was the time to go back.

She padded back to the hut, easing her pareu over her breasts. He looked up as she stepped on to the veranda. He'd set the table for two, lit a candle, and two bowls of thick green soup were placed each side of it. He hadn't started, but was waiting for her.

Miranda sat down and reluctantly spooned a mouthful. She closed her eyes in ecstasy. It was quite delicious. When she opened her eyes he was smiling across at her.

'It's good,' she murmured.

'My West Indian housekeeper taught me how to make it. It's one of my favourite dishes.'

They ate in silence, Miranda's brain working in a rush. She wanted to know, now, all about him, why he had come to help her, how he knew she was here.

'I've been thinking. You're right, I can't go on living here, hiding myself away from society. I'll have to go back some time and find a job so it might as well be now. I'll leave with Varga when he calls next.' She raised her brown eyes to his and was about to ask how he knew she was here when he started to shake his head.

'That's not necessary. We'll leave first thing in the morning.'

Miranda shifted uncomfortably in her rickety chair. 'Look, it's very kind of you to offer to take me off but I've got to make my own plans...'

'It's not kind of me at all. I have no choice...'

'No choice?' Miranda echoed, apprehension blossoming inside her.

He seemed reluctant to expand on that and when he eventually did she understood why. 'You're part of a deal I made with your uncle.' He laid his spoon down by the side of his empty plate, studied her across the flickering flame of the candle. His facial muscles were taut and unyielding.

'D—deal?' She couldn't come up with anything more than a feeble echo of his words.

'I was telling the truth when I told you this island is mine. In fact they all belong to me, all four of them. I bought them from your uncle a year before he was arrested.'

Miranda held her breath, some strange feminine intuition telling her there was more, much more.

'And?' she uttered weakly.

'And you were part of the deal,' he told her quietly.

Miranda's eye was caught by a firefly. She averted her eyes from him—anything rather than meet the cold, calculating measure of his. She was part of a deal, some sort of crazy transaction. She studied the firefly, marvelled at the miracle of it glowing in the dark . . . anything but take this man seriously.

'The net was closing in on your uncle and he knew it. His first concern was for your welfare. His business empire in the States kept you apart most of your life but that didn't stop him from loving you . . .'

'I know that!' Miranda retorted. 'I don't need to hear that from a stranger . . .'

'Don't get upset, Miranda.' Mendoza's voice was suddenly soft and warm and Miranda tried to relax. She sensed he'd been a friend of her uncle's; he must have been to know he cared for his orphaned niece. 'I'm trying to be as tactful as I can,' he went on.

Miranda steeled herself. You were usually tactful over something unpleasant. 'Go on,' she murmured.

'Your uncle sold me those islands on condition I took you along with them.'

She laughed then, a short, sharp, hysterical cry that vanished the firefly from sight. 'Don't be so ridiculous! I'm not a wife to be bargained for with a herd of cows or sheep, or islands in this case.'

'Marriage doesn't come into this. I'd never have agreed to the deal if that had been the case,' he said solemnly.

A misguided sense of insult stabbed at her. 'I'm glad to hear that,' Miranda croaked. 'It would have had to have been a posthumous wedding 'cos I'd rather die than marry you!'

He ignored that, fingered his spoon nervously. The small gesture brought Miranda down to earth. He wasn't enjoying this either.

'I bought four islands and a year of your life. A year in which the terms of the agreement state that I finish your education in any way I deem necessary and head you in the right direction to be able to cope with the rest of your life on your own. You will live with me on my island of San Paolo and . . .'

'No! No way!' Miranda screamed, jumping to her feet. 'This is *my* life! Not yours or my uncle's! He couldn't, he wouldn't do this to me!'

'He's done it, Miranda, and, before you explode once again, bear in mind one thought.' His eyes were implacable, cold and as jet as million-year-old coal under the Arctic. 'I don't like the idea any more than you do, but I wanted those islands, and you for a year was a small price to pay to get them. Keep that in mind when you feel hard done by. You belong to me, Miranda, for a year of your life and mine, and there is nothing either of us can do about it!'

CHAPTER TWO

STUNNED, Miranda gazed at Mendoza through un-flickering lashes. Tied to this man for a year of her life? It wasn't possible. Her uncle cared for her, had always given her the best. This man was a nothing. She couldn't be expected to take this seriously.

'I won't go with you,' she stated firmly. 'My re-fusal will break the contract. You'll lose the islands and I'll have my freedom.'

'I'm not prepared to lose those islands,' he re-plied, equally firmly. 'You're coming with me, willingly or unwillingly. The choice is yours. Do you have any coffee?'

'Coffee? How can you think of coffee at a time like this?' Miranda blurted. 'You've bought my life! You're forcing me into a situation I don't want!'

He stood up to go inside the shack. 'No, I haven't any coffee!' she called out to him. Seconds later he came back with the jug of mango juice and two glasses.

'It won't be so bad, Miranda. I live on a beauti-ful island, live well . . .'

'It will be a prison, none the less. And how are you supposed to finish my education? I know all I need to know to get a decent job in the States. Or

I could go back to England, where I was educated. What can you teach me that I don't already know?'

'That's a loaded question if ever there was one,' he smirked.

'If that smirk refers to sex,' she spat viciously, 'you couldn't teach me a thing!'

'Know it all, do you?'

Her cheeks flamed. Presler had been her only tutor, always given her star marks for her efforts, but somehow she felt she had failed the last paper dismally. She didn't answer Louis Mendoza because she was afraid of giving her naïveté away. She didn't doubt that he could teach her the *Karma Sutra* from beginning to end and beyond. Already he had fired her senses above anything she had ever experienced with Presler.

'Are you really going to carry this threat through?' she murmured. The candle was guttering low and she could scarcely see his face in the sultry darkness.

'It isn't a threat. I made a deal with your uncle…'

'He's in prison and won't know if you don't go through with the transaction.'

'That isn't the point. I made a promise and I'm going to honour it.'

'Honour among thieves is the saying, isn't it?' she said bitterly.

'I take exception to that,' he said quietly. 'I've never been a part of his organisation…'

'You've traded with him, though! Bought islands that were probably purchased in the first place to launder his dirty money. For all I know you

might be the Godfather of the Windward Isles and
sold my uncle down the river!'

Anger steeled him. Miranda noted the tightening
of the muscles at his throat. He could be aroused
to the point of murder, she realised. Maybe she had
hit the right chord and he was one of the syndicate
her uncle had been rumoured to associate with.

His voice was hostile yet controlled when he
spoke. 'I've never felt the need to answer to anyone
in my life before, but accusations like that from an
unkempt, arrogant, spoilt bitch I won't take. I come
from clean Portuguese stock, have lived on the
islands all my life, and don't trade with criminals...'

'That's a contradiction. You already have!'

'My conscience is clear. Not all of his organisation was outside of the law. I bought legitimately
owned islands from your uncle and the money I
paid him has gone into a trust fund for you...'

A gasp escaped from Miranda's lips at that. It
had crossed her mind that her uncle might have
made provision for her future but she had never
thought beyond surmise because she would have
refused it anyway. It was hard enough to accept
that her past had been bought from the proceeds
of goodness knew how many crooked deals.

'I don't want it!' she hissed through tight lips.
'I don't want any more of my uncle's black money!'
She stood up, went to the veranda and gripped the
warm wood tightly. She flinched when Mendoza
came and stood next to her.

'It isn't black money, it's your right—your pot
of gold at the end of the rainbow,' he told her

smoothly. 'One year under my care and then the fortune is yours.'

Tightening her grip on the rail, Miranda tilted her head back till her raven hair cascaded down her back and caught in the warm breeze. She started to laugh, softly, shaking her head from side to side in disbelief. 'That's it, is it? Offer me a rainbow and I'll dance to your and my uncle's tune?'

Slowly she turned to the man standing next to her, all laughter gone from her face. 'No chance, no chance whatsoever, Mendoza. I don't want his money, now or ever. This arrogant, spoilt bitch never learned to dance but she learned to survive on her own terms.'

'Very high and mighty,' he breathed next to her, standing so close she felt his heat and smelled the sea on his body. 'But ideals like that don't fill your bank account. You've led a sheltered, pampered, cushioned life, Miranda. Now you have nothing. No home...'

'I'll go to the condominium in Miami...'

'It was one of your uncle's assets frozen by the courts, as was the Long Island estate in America. You have nothing, Miranda, nothing but that scrap of scarlet you are wearing.'

It was true, but he wasn't to know how true. In a fit of pique just before leaving the penthouse in Miami she had disposed of all her designer outfits, sold her jewellery for a pittance to an unscrupulous dealer, just about raked up enough to pay for her flight down to St Vincent with enough over to buy Varga's services for a while. She'd even left her

Mercedes parked in the Miami court-house car park when the guilty verdict on her uncle had been announced.

She had run, panicked to get down to the tiny island she had loved as a child. A sanctuary to lick her wounds, a place unpressured by outside influences, a place to re-evaluate her life. And now this man had come to entice her back into it again. She didn't want it, the money, the lifestyle; she didn't want any of it ever again!

'I've survived here,' she murmured at last. 'It wasn't easy . . . it isn't easy, but somehow I made it.' She turned to him, her eyes glistening with unshed tears. 'I'm pretty proud of myself if no one else is. I know where I'm going, Mendoza, and it's not with you.' She turned and went inside the hut.

He didn't follow. She heard the creak of the old cane chair as he sat outside on the veranda, as if settling down for a long night's vigil.

Miranda untied her pareu and hung it on a hook on the wall next to her bunk. She lay down on the bed and pulled a sheet up over her. Sleep was impossible. She positioned her head so she could see him through the open door, see him when he left for his yacht. She lay as still as possible—to toss and turn generated heat and it was uncomfortably hot as it was.

He wasn't going to go. She'd watched him for hours, sleeping in the chair, his long, muscular legs propped up on the table. He must be in agony. She turned to the wooden wall and closed her eyes. He'd be gone by first light.

*   *   *

The next morning Miranda strolled lazily up to the pool with a bucket for fresh water to rinse her hair with after her morning swim. The sea and sun had played havoc with her once lush, glossy tresses. Already the sun was high and scorching heaven and earth.

He'd gone, and so had the yacht. Miranda's relief was enormous. Now she could think clearly, make her own plans for the future without any interference from him.

The waterfall fascinated her, fed from an underwater stream further up the island, and the water gushed clear and cool. She was tempted to shower away the heat of the night but her fear of the dark, menacing pool below it stopped her. She'd swim as usual in the bay and then rinse herself with the fresh water.

'Yuck!' Her first bucket of water scooped from the pool was alive with some sort of larvae. She tipped it away, skirted the edge of the pool to lean across and fill the bucket with fresh water from under the waterfall.

But Miranda lost her grip on the rock as she leaned over, and grazed her shoulder as she went down. Her lips were apart as she hit the water, in a half-uttered scream of fright. Almost immediately the fissure in the rock dragged at her legs and she kicked out, panicking as she was sucked against the jagged rock. Her last breath was expelled from her lungs as hands grabbed hers and she was dragged, barely conscious, from the pool.

Miranda retched, tightened her grip on the arms that had saved her and finally blinked open her eyes.

'Don't struggle, you're going to be just fine.'

'Mendoza!' she gasped, then cried out in agony and grasped at her raw shoulder.

'Easy, easy. You might have put it out.' He held her arm with one hand, her shoulder with the other. She thought he was going to wrench her apart as if she were a wishbone but he let out a gravelled sigh of relief and let her go. 'Just a graze, everything where it should be.'

'Except you! You shouldn't be here!' She tried to get to her feet, groaned as blood oozed from a long graze down her shin.

He lifted her up into his arms then and carried her down to the shack and laid her on the bunk. So shaken with her narrow escape, she let him untie her wet pareu and ease it away from her skin. He covered her with the crumpled sheet without looking at her body.

'Rest a while; I'll get some clean water to bathe those wounds. I don't suppose you have an antiseptic lotion here?'

Miranda shook her head. Hardly one of her priorities when she'd come here. An oversight she had regretted on numerous occasions. Till she had built up an immunity to avaricious insects she had suffered terribly with bites and stings.

She lay in agony waiting for him to return; her shoulder and leg throbbed painfully but worse was the realisation that she appeared a capricious child in his eyes. Even her naked body had failed to arouse any interest in him and yet last night his mouth had shown positively feverish interest.

'Yes, you fool,' she murmured to herself as she got up from the bed and hobbled to the dressing-table drawer for a clean cotton shirt. 'He was teaching you a salutary lesson in playing with fire... Don't!'

'I thought I told you to rest?'

She finished buttoning her shirt as he loped into the shack with a bucket of water.

'I'm all right.'

'You're not—there's blood oozing on to your shirt already.'

She twisted her head to look at the dark stain spreading across her shoulder. Stupid. She shivered, not knowing why, weakly tried to fidget out of the shirt...

And now she had fainted, her muzzy head told her as she came round, on the bunk again, the sheet covering her breasts. Her shoulder and leg felt more comfortable now, covered in strips of clean cotton. He must have bathed them while she was out cold.

'I suppose I ought to throw a fit of hysterics now and then you will know for sure I'm not quite right in the head,' she murmured, feeling weak and foolish. She watched him move around the room, for the first time noticing he wasn't wearing the faded Bermudas but fresh white shorts and espadrilles, neither wet, so he couldn't have swum ashore. His beard was even more prominent this morning—not blue-black but a curious dark red colour.

'I know it for sure already,' he uttered as he gathered her few personal belongings into a card-board box. 'And you're stubborn, reckless, totally selfish...'

'Haven't you anything good to say about me?'

'You have a beautiful body,' he casually stated without looking at her.

Miranda bit her lip. She'd asked for that. 'Which goes to prove where your interests lie,' she baited, not sure why but finding it irresistible anyway.

He smiled, emptied the contents of the dressing-table drawer into the box. 'A Jersey cow has a beautiful body too, but I don't want to bed one.'

Her colour rose. 'I w-wasn't suggesting——'

'I should hope not,' he cut in. 'So long as you keep our relationship strictly on a business level you shouldn't have any problems.'

'*Me* any problems?' Miranda spluttered, trying to sit up. She held the sheet tightly around her in case he thought she was making *another* pass at him.

'Do you want these shells?'

Miranda was grateful for the change of subject. 'Yes...just a minute, what do you think you're doing?' It suddenly hit her that he was packing for her.

'Collecting all your bits and pieces together. I want you to feel at home on San Paola...'

'I thought I'd made myself clear on that subject. I'm not going with you!'

He faced her then, that bored look on his face. He said quietly yet firmly, 'And I'd thought I'd made myself quite clear too. You will do as you're told and stop acting like a selfish child.'

'That's the second time you've called me selfish . . .'

'Not without reason.' His eyes darkened and he stepped towards her. 'Do you have one iota of feeling in that beautiful head of yours? Or is it simply stuffed full of poor-me-aren't-I-hard-done-by clichés? How about giving a thought to your uncle instead of yourself for a change? You might find you like the feeling of caring for someone other than Miranda Gordon!'

Flushing hotly, Miranda struggled to her feet, swayed, but he made no attempt to assist her. She righted herself before gushing out, 'And what is that supposed to mean?'

'You haven't contacted your uncle since you've been here.'

'I wrote to him before I left Miami. Told him about my fiancé rejecting me, told him exactly where I was going and why . . .'

'And nothing more since then. He's worried about you.'

'How do you know?'

'Because I was with him last week. He wrote and asked me to go and see him and I did.'

Miranda slumped back down on the bunk. 'How is he?' she murmured, her eyes searching his.

He raised a satisfied brow. 'So you do care after all.'

'I never said I didn't. My uncle knows that. He would understand why I had to come here, too.'

Louis's tone softened. 'That's why he left you alone to get over all this, but three months is long enough, Miranda. He wants to put into operation our agreement now—wants you off this island and into my care.'

'Why you?' Miranda cried. Her uncle could have assigned her to any number of people but this mean man.

Louis levelled his dark eyes at her. 'Because your uncle couldn't trust anyone else. Everyone close to him, in business and his personal life, turned against him when things in Miami began to hot up. He knew his downfall was imminent. I'd approached him about the islands a long time back. He seemed to like me. He saw in me a stranger he trusted, the opportunity to provide for your future if anything happened to him. I liked your uncle enough to agree to his conditions.'

'Liar! You wanted the islands!' Miranda burst out. 'You'd have agreed to anything to get your hands on them! You call me selfish! You don't care about me...'

'No, I don't! I don't like you very much either!' he grated back, silencing her with the brutality of his words. 'But I'm willing to try. What about you? You've spent three months of your life martyring yourself out here without a thought for the worry you are putting your uncle through——' He stopped suddenly, pummelled his forehead with his fingers, regretting his whiplash outburst. 'I'm sorry. I know what your uncle has put you through too. I know it hasn't been easy for you...'

'It hasn't, but I don't need you to smooth the next year of my life, thank you,' Miranda told him tightly. 'I'm not a child and I'm not helpless.'

'Why are you so against me?' he interrupted, eyes boring into hers.

Miranda gaped up at him. Why indeed? Fear, maybe. She hadn't given it much thought but he was attractive and the last thing she wanted was to fall in love with another man when the last had hurt her so badly. But no, no risk of that. He wasn't her type at all—far too pushy. No, it was more than that. He raised her hackles far too easily to contemplate living on his island with him for a year.

'I'm not against you personally,' she lied. 'I just want to do my own thing. I'm quite capable of it, you know.' She widened her dark eyes plaintively. 'I've survived on my own here, found my own food——'

He cut her down before she could go on extolling her virtues. 'An imbecile could survive on this island,' he interjected coldly. 'There's fresh water here. You haven't had to bore for it. There's an abundance of bread-fruit, papaw, mangoes. You might be a crack-shot with your uncle's rifle but I doubt you've had the guts to shoot the odd scrap of wildlife.'

True, she hadn't. She wouldn't have killed anything furry or feathery if her life had depended on it. 'I've fished, caught crabs with my bare hands!' Miranda protested. And that had been bad enough, having to strike dead a wriggling fish, and the crab, *the* crab, she had let go, not been able to face plunging it into hot water.

'A blind man can fish these waters; the fish practically come out and lie at your feet . . .'

'OK, know-all! But there aren't many women who would have done what I've done. It's eerie here at night. Anyone could have landed here and raped—or murdered—me!'

'You've been here before, know this island is impossible to land on——'

'You did!'

'Because I know it, know there is a treacherous coral reef out there that only an experienced swimmer can negotiate.'

'Rubbish! Varga brings my supplies to the other side of the island, the Atlantic side. Anyone could have landed there to take advantage of me.' She realised then that that was where he had moved his yacht to, changed his clothes and come ashore. The rough, rugged shore where only experience and knowledge of the currents and moods of the turbulent waters counted.

'Only a native of the islands would take such a risk on the Atlantic side, and you have nothing to fear from the local islanders and you know it,' he insisted.

'Why are you so determined to put me down?' she uttered weakly, pulling the sheet around her more firmly.

'Because you ask for it,' he returned coolly.

He came closer towards her and she shrank away from him, pressing the backs of her legs against the bunk to give herself strength. 'You seem to think you've done something special here, proved you're not the pampered little rich girl the world has dealt a rough blow to. If you want to prove your toughness get out into the real world. It's more of a jungle out there than it is on this wild island.'

She blurted hotly, 'I know that and I'm not seeking any medals for what I've done, but I want the chance to make my own way...'

'Miranda.' He took her shoulders, held them so gently and persuasively that she nearly fell into his arms. In that instant she wanted to go with him, would have gone with anyone, not just him, because now she was exhausted, physically, mentally, in every way. 'You need this year with me, you need time to get adjusted. Now you are over the hurt of your fiancé's rejection, your uncle's misdealings. You've had time to cope with those feelings, but there's more. You've never had a job, have you?'

She lowered her lashes, shook her head dismally. 'I finished my education in Switzerland last year. The school was so exclusive the sort of girls that went there weren't expected to earn a living. I know how to organise a cocktail party...'

He pulled her into his arms and held her head against his shoulder, as a father would do to a child. She felt him tremble against her, with laughter not passion.

'I don't see what's so funny,' she husked.

'It isn't funny but it is, if you know what I mean.' He eased her away from him to look down into her flushed face. 'So Robina Crusoe can organise a cocktail party.' He tilted her chin. 'Can't you see the irony of it?'

She nodded her head and forced a smile to her pale lips. If he was trying to make her see the idiocy of her ways, he was succeeding. She felt ridiculously small and vulnerable.

'It would be brave of you to try and get a job and support yourself, but you have nowhere to live, don't even know for sure what you want to do or where you want to do it. I'll help you, Miranda.'

His hand came up and smoothed her hair and she let him. She would go with him, too, because she did need help, needed it more in that moment than she had ever done in her life. She wasn't about to go soft in the head, though. She knew why Louis Mendoza was doing this. He had no choice. He was as trapped in this situation as she was. So long as she didn't lose sight of that she would be all right. She would think of it as a business arrangement as he'd suggested and everything would be just fine.

He helped her down into the boat, a tricky operation, since the lovely yacht bucked in the fierce seas as she tried to get aboard from the rocks close to where he had anchored.

She suppressed a cry of pain as he grasped her tightly round the waist and hoisted her to the deck. The man didn't know his own strength. He helped her below to where air-conditioning purred. It was the first cool place she'd been in since the hotel in Miami during the trial. She sat down on the cool leather upholstery and let out a sigh of pleasure.

'I'll make some coffee when we're on automatic pilot; just relax till we're on our way.'

He left her below deck and as the engine roared she stared stoically at her entwined fingers in her lap. She couldn't look out of the porthole, didn't want to take a last look at the island which had offered her sanctuary in her months of need. She had loved and hated it equally and, even now, accepting Louis Mendoza's help, she still wasn't sure if she was doing the right thing by leaving it. She had been free there, freer than at any other time in her life. Such freedom would never happen again. Maybe she had been selfish, totally absorbed in herself, not giving a thought to her uncle, but at the time she had felt only the pain and the hurt and the disgrace.

Later, her mouth started to water uncontrollably as Mendoza brewed coffee in the galley. The aroma was like an aphrodisiac to her starved senses.

'You were anchored out in the bay for two days before you came ashore,' she said as he handed her a mug of coffee. 'Why?'

'Soul-searching, I suppose.' He sat across the cabin, his long legs stretched out in front of him, his dark colouring contrasting so markedly with the white interior. She supposed she might be about the same colour after three months almost naked on the island. She hadn't had a mirror, her only

guide to her appearance the clear turquoise of the
sea and the menacing green of the pool.

'You feel guilty about what you're doing?' she
suggested, holding his eyes. He must do—it was
tantamount to kidnapping.

He looked away. 'I'm not happy with the arrangement and sorry to disillusion you, but for my
own sake, not yours. I lead a full business life and
you will be an encumbrance I can do without at
the moment.'

Miranda felt inexplicably hurt by that. He read
it in her eyes as he glanced back at her.

'I'm sorry, that sounded very cruel. I don't want
to hurt you any more than you have been already.
I'll do my best for you, Miranda. For your sake
and your uncle's.' He said it kindly, paternally. For
some reason Miranda didn't like that.

'That hasn't completely answered my question;
why didn't you come ashore straight away?'

Another question he was slow in giving an answer
to. 'I wanted to observe you,' he said after draining
his coffee. 'See what I was about to lumber myself
with.'

'At least you're honest!' she retorted. 'So you
would have up-anchored and fled if I hadn't met
with your approval?'

'You don't meet with my approval,' he drawled,
holding her astonished gaze this time. 'It was the
reason I was so hesitant, the reason it took me two
days to make that decision. I watched you in that
time. Swimming in the bay, gathering shells on the

shore, watching me watching you. You're a very sexy child-woman——'

'You said I was hardly gaol-bait material!' Miranda interrupted, deeply embarrassed by his sudden revelations.

'At the moment,' he grated meaningfully. 'But I guess after a while in a civilised environment, with meat to flesh out your body and a decent haircut, you could turn out to be a stunner. I know potential when I see it and that can spell danger.'

'D-danger?' Miranda croaked. Oh, if only he had come out with this on the island. She wouldn't have come, definitely not!

He laughed then. How she hated it when he laughed at her. He stood up. 'Yes, danger,' he said softly, leaning down to tuck a lock of hair behind her ear. 'I could get to want you as much as you want me and when you get to my island you'll find out just how dangerous that can be for both of us!'

Miranda opened her mouth to abuse him with the strongest invectives she could muster, but they froze on her lips as he stepped past her and climbed the steps to the deck.

Numbly fixed to the white leather upholstery, she sat motionless, her lips slightly apart with shock. He hadn't been teaching her a salutary lesson last night; he *had* wanted her when he had kissed her so passionately and, worse, he had recognised the need in her. Realised that her come-on had just been a sham. And it had been a sham, only now could she admit to that. She had needed him last night, wanted him to make love to her, a build-up of frustrated emotions her exile had forced upon her. But didn't he realise that any other attractive man would have had the same effect on her after such a long time on her own? Nothing at all to do with him personally!

Miranda stood up and tottered to the shower-room off the main cabin. The boat suddenly hit bad water and tossed perilously. She clung to the tower-rail and swivelled to look at herself in the full-length mirror. She could hardly believe what she was seeing. No cool, sophisticated Miranda Gordon stared back at her, but a stranger, a dark bronzed stranger with such a wild, native look in her eyes that she rubbed at them viciously. Her eyebrows needed plucking, her sun-ravaged hair was dull with split ends and yet there were golden-red streaks, bleached by the sun, rippling among the raven.

She'd lost weight, horribly so. With shaking fingers she fumbled with the knot of her pareu, let it slide to the floor to reveal her nudity. Her colouring was the same all over, deep golden brown. Even her nipples had darkened to deep brown aureoles. Her once soft curves had sharpened, she looked lean and hard, had a youth's body now, not a woman's. Her breasts were smaller, surely. She touched them, caressed them and felt that terrible need blossom deep inside her. She pressed her hands against the mirror, lowered her head so she couldn't look at herself again.

Mendoza had said she had a beautiful body. He had lied. She hated herself, hated what she had done to herself, and more than anything she hated this feeling inside her. This ache for a man she didn't even like, who'd admitted he didn't like her! A man who had control of the next year of her life!

CHAPTER THREE

LOUIS MENDOZA gazed down at the sleeping form curled foetus-like on the leather seating below deck. She was beautiful, exciting and trouble with a capital T.

He wanted to reach out and caress her mass of turbulent raven hair, to smooth his fingers over her bronzed silken cheeks. He wanted her with an urgency he hadn't experienced since his teens. But at thirty-four he recognised his lust for what it was. An elemental need. Nothing more, nothing less. One that could be and would be suppressed simply because of its foolhardiness.

He frowned. This coiled scrap of sensuality had aggravated the doubts he was already battling with. His weakness last night had served as a warning, though—one he wasn't about to ignore.

But what about her? This fragile bloom with a dangerous fire smouldering deep within her, this tormented soul who didn't know what she wanted or where she was going. She had flamed in his arms last night, exposed her raw need with such a painful naïveté that he would have been a bastard to have pursued it any further. And he had been tempted, agonisingly so.

Silently he cursed Sagan Gordon for bringing this on him. The older man had tied him up so tightly in the island deal that he'd had no choice but to go through with it. Not for a minute had he imagined the niece he had agreed to watch over for a year would turn out to be such a stunning liability. Somehow he had thought it would be easy to set her on her feet again, but it wasn't going to be, he knew that with a grave certainty. Served him right for being so damned ambitious, wanting to expand his already crowded horizons. He should have left her and those accursed islands to lap in the Caribbean for ever more.

'Miranda.' He touched her good shoulder and she started, opened her wide eyes as fearfully as a young fawn woken by the step of a predator. 'We're home. Welcome to San Paola.'

Sleep cleared from her muzzy head. She sat up as he turned away from her to climb the short flight of steps to the deck. She was here, her prison for the next year. She shuddered, swung her long legs to the ground and followed him up into the hot sun.

They were moored to a long jetty that jutted out from an exquisite bay. Sea as calm as stretched blue silk, sand as white and pure as angels' wings. A creamy white low-slung villa spread out before her, nearly melding to the beach but for a strip of emerald-green lawn and a group of swaying fan palms separating the two. Pristine luxury that would have torn a gasp of pleasure from Miranda's lips if it weren't for the fact that she had no choice but to stay here.

'Pentonville paradise,' she murmured to herself, clutching her cardboard box to her chest and stepping out of the yacht on to the wooden jetty. Louis took the box from her and she followed her gaoler as he strode along the wooden slats to the beach.

The sand was unbearably hot under her bare feet and she hurried to the welcome coolness of the thick savannah lawn.

'I'll introduce you to the staff and let your personal maid settle you in,' Louis clipped, not turning to look at her. 'I'm afraid I won't have much time for you today. I have work to catch up on.'

She was hating it already, feeling a nuisance and an encumbrance.

'Louis, darling! You're back!'

The shrill voice came from the other end of the wide veranda that ran the length of the villa, all doors opening on to it. Louis and Miranda both swung round to face the caller.

A wife! was Miranda's first strangled thought. She hadn't anticipated that—not after what had happened between her and Mendoza. Her heart beat erratically and then she observed as if she weren't really there, and that was exactly how the lovely pale blonde made her feel.

The blonde embraced Louis Mendoza, averted her delicate cheek from the roughness of his beard with a demure movement which for some reason gave Miranda a prickle of satisfaction.

'Honestly, darling, did you have to take so long? You've been away for days. Missed Hazel's dinner party last night. What was the problem? I thought it was going to be quite straightforward, there and back in a day.' There was an edge to her tone that Miranda picked up on but Louis seemed oblivious to.

'Miranda had a slight accident and needed some rest before we set out...'

Miranda swallowed the protest before it came to fruition on her lips. That was a lie, but why? She had no time to analyse that before cool blue eyes were upon her for the first time.

'Miranda Gordon, Catherine de Vaux,' Louis Mendoza delivered with cool indifference.

She wasn't his wife. But why the blazes was Miranda so relieved? She tried to smile but her dry lips bared across her teeth as the controlled gaze that met hers showed that Miranda wasn't at all what the icy blonde was expecting.

'So pleased to meet you,' came the insincere words masked with honey and spice.

Louis had the nerve to smile. Miranda picked up bad vibes. She hadn't expected this—another woman and one who had such assurance that she guessed she was an integral part of Mendoza's life. So what? It was a shock, that was all.

The cool eyes went no further than Miranda's face and for that she was grateful. She felt a mess in her crumpled pareu, with her battered shoulder, bare brown legs with that unsightly graze down her shin and naked feet stained green from the moist lawn.

Catherine, in contrast, was the sophisticated designer-draped, voluptuous feline that once had been Miranda Gordon, though Miranda wondered if she had been that cool, distant and well endowed. Was it any wonder Mendoza had scorned her so when his taste lay with such full-blown beauty?

Miranda couldn't summon so much as a how-do-you-do. Louis sensed her discomfort and winged his attention to Catherine.

'Could you organise some lunch with Naomi, darling? We'll take it by the poolside. And send Sunset along to the guest suite to settle Miranda in. I'll show Miranda where everything is and then get myself cleaned up before joining you.'

Catherine smiled and squeezed his arm, a gesture Miranda felt was aimed at her—affection with a liberal powdering of possession. 'Then I can welcome you home properly,' she teased, running a pert finger over his beard. She turned away and on tiny gold heels clipped in the opposite direction, her violet silk sundress wafting lightly around her slender alabaster legs.

'Then I can welcome you home properly,' Miranda mimicked in a small, simpering voice as they continued along the endless veranda.

'You can cut that out!' Louis frosted, a sudden frown darkening his brow.

Miranda wondered at that look. Guilty conscience for having made a pass or two at her when he had the lovely Catherine tucked far away at home?

'Who is she?' Miranda couldn't contain her curiosity any longer.

'Catherine de Vaux, of the de Vaux of Florida,' was the only unsatisfactory answer he was prepared to give her. Miranda accepted it silently, for the time being.

Miranda's accommodation was at the end of the veranda. Sliding patio doors opened to the bedroom and another door across the room opened into the main house. Louis showed her the small dressing-room and the en-suite bathroom linked to it.

It was all coolly furnished in pale yellow and soft pinks with white louvred wardrobes and cupboards and slubbed silk chairs to recline in. The bathroom was a dream of frosty white and brass, mirrored walls and marbled floor. Slatted white blinds at the windows and patio doors shaded and protected the rooms from the torrid heat of the sun.

'It's lovely,' Miranda said quietly, padding around the room, touching, exploring.

Louis stood watching her, leaning against the patio doors. When he spoke his voice was oddly gravelled. 'You have everything you want here...'

'Everything but my freedom!' Miranda jerked out. She loved her accommodation, knew she would love everything else here on the island, but...

'It isn't a prison, Miranda. There's a car in the garage for you.'

'Another part of the deal!'

He ignored that. 'There are new clothes for you in the wardrobe——'

'Stop it!' she shrieked, turning her back on him, clutching at her shoulders. 'I'm not a damned waif!'

She felt his presence behind her, his warmth, his smell. He touched her lightly on her upper arms, avoiding her grazed shoulder. The touch turned to a caress, burning into her flesh like a branding iron.

'I want you to be happy here,' he murmured.

'Why?' She jerked round to face him, unable to bear his closeness a second longer. His hands dropped to his side. 'Surely it doesn't matter if I'm happy or not? We both have to suffer this year. You because you made a deal and me because I haven't anything else.'

His eyes looked so pained that Miranda lowered her lashes in shame. He was doing his best, though the motives could hardly be spurred by compassion or the remotest of feelings for her.

'Don't make the situation any more difficult than it is,' he said softly. 'Stop fighting me and all should be well.'

Her head shot up at that. Why did she get the feeling he was fighting some inner battle too? Of course he was; she was but a thorn in his side with the lovely Catherine around. Her eyes settled on his beard. He was about to clean himself up for the blonde, but hadn't bothered before, no, not for her! The thought was unreasonable but nevertheless there.

'I'm sorry,' she offered at last. She was acting like the spoilt brat he assumed she was. 'I'll do my best not to rock your boat.'

'No fear of that,' he murmured and she wondered if that was a thinly veiled resolve like the warning he had pressed on her earlier. Was Catherine de Vaux the danger for them both?

Her heart felt like a cube of Arctic ice inside her. Frozen by the thought that the blonde was someone big in his life and she was going to be in the way. Another reason for him to feel the weight of his responsibility, to regret the deal he had made out of greed for her uncle's islands.

'What do you expect of me?' she asked tentatively. 'I mean, what am I supposed to do with myself all day?'

'For the moment, nothing. I suggest you rest——'

'I've rested for three months!' she blurted, then bit her lip despondently. She wasn't even trying!

'It will take you a few days to settle, to find your way around,' he went on as if she hadn't uttered a word. 'Catherine will be here to help. She'll introduce you to the other islanders.'

That was the last thing Miranda wanted but she tightened a grip on her protestations. He was passing the buck to Catherine, and who could blame him? She didn't know what he did for a living but to support this place it had to be something heavyweight, and he wasn't about to allow her to disrupt his schedule. Her life here would be no different from life with her uncle—because of his business empire he'd had no time for her either.

There was a soft movement outside on the veranda and they both turned.

'Sunset,' Louis called and a young West Indian girl, barefooted and dressed in a simple floral housedress, walked hesitantly into the room and smiled.

It was the first genuine, open smile Miranda had seen so far. The tension inside her eased.

'This is Miss Miranda, Sunset. I want you to look after her and make her feel at home. When she's settled bring her out to the pool for lunch.' He turned and left them both and Miranda could sense his relief. She stemmed her irritation and smiled at the girl.

They got on well, immediately, which was a relief to Miranda and probably to the girl who had been assigned to serve her.

'I'll show you how the shower works,' Sunset smiled, 'and then I'll unpack for you.'

She showed no outward sign of curiosity at the cardboard box crammed with her meagre belongings which Louis had dumped at the foot of the bed, and Miranda felt no need to explain. That was the ease of their new relationship.

It was the most glorious shower Miranda had ever experienced, the most glorious hair-washing session. Shampoo *and* conditioner. She wrung the experience for all it was worth, relished every delicious second of it. She stepped from the shower glowing with new life. Already her grazes were less sore and she smoothed body lotion over her tanned limbs, a luxury that three months' exile was almost worth waiting for.

'I'll comb your hair for you,' Sunset smiled and together they went out on to the veranda. Miranda seated herself in a cane chair, a towel wrapped around her body, and let Sunset sort out her tangled mass of hair.

Jasmine scented the air, bright cerise bougain-villaea sprawled up the veranda posts, humming-birds hovered in the nucleus of vibrant hibiscus flowers. Miranda had been in some luxurious homes in her time—school holidays had been spent with a nanny in the penthouse in Miami and the old colonial Long Island mansion—but nothing compared to the peace and tranquillity of this lovely villa. Perhaps if she tried very hard she could settle and benefit from being here. But what to do with her time? Just surviving on El Paraiso had filled the day. Here there were servants; sweet Sunset would be offended if she attempted to do anything for herself.

'You hair is very dry at the ends,' Sunset told her. 'Tomorrow I will oil it for you. Coconut oil is very good. I use it all the time.'

Miranda smiled. 'That would be nice,' she acknowledged.

When her hair was combed and nearly dry in the heat Sunset offered to show her around but Miranda gently insisted she would find her own way about. She wanted some breathing time of her own.

'The pool is at the front of the house, and lunch will be served there,' Sunset smiled, seemingly to understand her mood.

Did she know why she was here? Miranda wondered. She doubted it. Her uncle's notoriety wouldn't have reached these remote islands and would have made no impression on the local people if it had. She knew the Caribbean well enough to know that the islanders lived a very insular life.

Miranda stepped back into her bedroom when Sunset had gone, smiled at the sight of the shells she had collected on the sandy beach of El Paraiso, now so carefully arranged on the wide window-sills. Sunset had taken the cardboard box away with her, and a bundle of pareus to be washed, and there was little else left. The sum of her past life.

With a sigh Miranda padded to the dressing-room. But it had been her choice to scorn her past— one she didn't regret, though. She had never taken her cushioned life for granted, had always thought there must be something beyond the frippery her uncle's guilty conscience for not giving her more of his time had endowed her with. But she had been trapped in his way of life and now she was trapped in someone else's—Louis Mendoza's. It occurred to her she would have been trapped in Presler's life too if he hadn't rejected her. Maybe that had been a blessing. This situation definitely wasn't a blessing.

'Oh, no!' she groaned as she opened the wardrobe door to reveal a rail of new clothes. Miranda fingered them in surprise, examined the labels in disbelief. They all came from the exclusive boutique in Miami she had an account with. How had Louis Mendoza known that? Her uncle, maybe?

She slipped on a skirt of linen damask. It hung on her hips like a sack. Hopelessly too big. Her weight loss seemed greater than she had anticipated.

'Nothing fits!' she cried in dismay, kicking the clothes to the floor. She wanted her pareus back, a symbol of her new-found freedom and individuality. Tears of frustration welled in her eyes. If he thought he was trying to help, he wasn't! She felt worse than ever, more of a liability, more of a charity case! Why, oh, why hadn't he left her on her island?

With furious fingers she pulled on a print dress of fine cotton, so big it hung down off one shoulder. She looked at herself in the mirror. She looked like a bag of bones swathed in a designer duvet cover! And then she smiled. What did it matter? Wasn't this what she had been rebelling against, the finery her uncle's ill-gotten gains had provided her with? Now Mendoza was her benefactor and, if this was what he expected her to wear, so be it!

She didn't bother with the shoes and sandals neatly racked at the foot of the wardrobe. Her feet couldn't have shrunk but she had learned to love the freedom of bare feet, warm sand between her toes, spongy grass under her soles. She went outside into bright sunlight and started to find her way around, circling the villa and exploring the lush, beautifully kept gardens. There were emerald-green lawns, cactus gardens, a rose garden so heavy with scent she lingered, pressing her face to the heady blooms.

She lost track of time, till she heard voices, raised voices, well, one at least. Catherine's.

Miranda hesitated to go further than a clump of scented pink oleander. She could see the aquamarine of the pool ahead through the leathery green leaves of the shrub. She had almost circled the gardens surrounding the villa, arrived at the front of the house where the pool and tennis court lay. She could hear the voices but not see the perpetrators, but she was in no doubt that it was Louis and Catherine.

'The lunch is ruined——'

'Salad can't be ruined,' Louis interrupted calmly.

'It isn't the point. You said lunch by the pool and *she* isn't here. She'll run rings round you, Louis. Mark my words. I smelled trouble the minute I set eyes on her. She's a damned crook's niece, for God's sake. What more can you expect from her?'

Miranda went cold inside. This was what she had run from: tarred-with-the-same-brush syndrome. Her uncle's crimes were her own.

'You were a fool ever to get involved, islands or no damned islands. You should have steered clear of such a deal.'

'When I want your opinion, I'll ask for it,' Louis said quietly and so firmly that Catherine de Vaux changed tactics. Her voice changed to a pouting simper.

'I didn't mean anything, darling, but she's such a mess. She's been running wild like a native and it shows. Do you honestly expect me to traipse her round the island with me on my social calls? Hazel will have a fit. And once everyone knows who she is I'll be ostracised. Hazel's husband lost thousands on that Miami deal.'

'That has nothing to do with Miranda,' Louis stated.

'Mud sticks, darling. If she were a bit more refined she might get away with it, but she looks like a vagrant, all that wild hair...'

'She's been living rough,' Louis grazed. 'Poor kid didn't know which way to turn when they sentenced her uncle...'

Miranda didn't want to hear any more. She turned and ran, tears stinging her eyes, a curious buzzing in her ears. A mess! Vagrant! But it was the 'poor kid' that had really hurt. Not only was Mendoza locked into this arrangement but he felt sorry for her too!

She ran to the beach, panting with the effort of trying to hold back her tears. She didn't want anyone to see her crying; that would make it worse, much worse. She controlled herself, trailed her feet in the warm water and slowly headed to an outcrop of rocks on the opposite side of the bay to the jetty.

Slumping on cool sand in the shade, she held her throbbing head in her hands.

'Still running, Miranda? I thought that would stop once you were here.'

Miranda scuttled to her feet, was about to head anywhere out of his range, but Louis hauled her back, held her hands at her side.

'This has got to end, Miranda. This silly, childish attitude of yours, running when you don't like——' She opened her mouth to protest but he stilled the words on her lips by tightening his grip on her wrists. 'I saw you from the veranda. What is it this time? You don't like your room, you can't get on with Sunset . . . ?'

'No, it's you!' she stormed, twisting her wrists hopelessly, her breath jerking from her parted lips. 'I overheard you talking with Catherine . . . the "mess" bit, the "vagrant" bit and worse, worse than all that, the "poor kid" bit! How do you think that makes me feel?' With a sharp wrench she flicked her wrist out of his hands, held her thumb and forefinger half an inch apart. 'That big, Mendoza. You make me feel *that* big!'

'You shouldn't have eavesdropped . . .'

'Oh, don't give me that old chestnut: no eavesdropper hears good of herself. The fact is I heard what you were saying and I'm glad. Now I know exactly what I'm up against. Five minutes back in your so-called civilisation and it's started. The fingers pointing . . .'

'No one is doing that to you,' he grated.

'Catherine is! Already she's panicking at the thought of introducing a crook's niece to her fancy friends. And what else was it?' Miranda rubbed her forehead. She couldn't think straight; all this rush and turmoil after her tranquil life on El Paraiso was addling her brain. 'Oh, yes.' She raised her wide dark eyes to his. 'Hazel's husband has lost thousands on the Miami deal. Well, I don't know what deal that was but it's painfully obvious it was one of my uncle's...'

'That has nothing to do with you.'

'Yes, so I believe you said,' Miranda hissed back sarcastically. 'But clever Catherine was right whereas you are hopelessly wrong. Mud sticks, Mendoza. Your friends might make a brave effort to accept me, for your sake, but deep down they will always hold my uncle's crimes against me. They wouldn't be able to help themselves. It's human nature.'

'And that's precisely what you'll have to face,' he argued. His fingers suddenly entwined in the hand he was still holding. 'But you'll have me beside you and that was your uncle's intention. He knew what you would have to go through before you could hold your head up.'

'I can do that without your help,' she iced. 'And let go of my hand!' She snatched it away and defied him with the narrowing of her eyes. 'I'm not a poor kid, I'm a woman, with feelings and needs.' Her voice lowered pleadingly. 'Let me go, Mendoza. Let me off this island.'

'To do what, to go where? You're not ready yet, Miranda. When you are, I'll let you go, don't worry. I've no intention of keeping you here against your will once you are on your feet.'

There was a curious catch in his voice and Miranda frowned up at him. He was clean-shaven now, his jet hair slicked back from his masterful forehead. The white shorts and espadrilles were exchanged for crisp linen trousers, a white short-sleeved shirt so fine she could see the hair on his chest through it, the darkness of his tanned skin. He looked sharp and successful even in the turbulent heat of the tropics. He looked the perfect partner for the sophisticated Catherine.

She leaned back against a high rock and lowered her gaze to the disturbed sand at her feet. It might have worked if *she* hadn't been here.

'You're in love with her, aren't you?' Bravely Miranda raised her head to take the full impact of his reply, sensing it would hurt but not knowing why and wondering if she really cared if the answer was positive anyway.

'I presume you mean Catherine,' he said, a small smile gathering at the corner of his mouth.

'Who else?' she murmured, heat and more heat threatening her throat. She cared; it was a horrible realisation. But maybe she was just being selfish again; with Catherine out of the way she might have a chance to rehabilitate herself. Mendoza didn't throw insults around about her relationship to her uncle.

'That's a very personal question.'

'Well, if I'm going to live here for a year we're going to get pretty personal anyway,' she threw back at him.

His hint of a smile blossomed into a sardonic grin. 'I wonder just how personal you're aiming for.'

The heat invaded her throat and flushed her face too. A poor choice of words she had emitted. Was he presuming it another come-on? So what? Push him to his limits and he might be glad to get rid of her.

'That depends on how personal *you* want to get,' she said pointedly.

'A very dangerous suggestion,' he said softly, his hand moving to her naked shoulder where her dress had slipped down. His caress was like fire on silk — inflammable. The heat raged through her, sparking the smouldering embers of her senses. 'Is this another of your tests? Playing your little games again?' he mocked as if she had let her dress slip for his benefit.

Her eyes slid to his hand on her shoulder. 'You're the one playing games, Mendoza,' she husked. 'You warned me of the dangers here on your island, yet you don't heed the warnings yourself. Is Catherine the danger?'

His hand seemed to freeze to her flesh for a second and then it softened again. 'No, we are the danger, to ourselves. It's exciting and fun to play with fire but if you get caught the burns can scar you for life.'

Miranda forced a smile to her dry lips. 'I believe you are side-tracking. Catherine is the danger, not us. She calls you darling, she hates me because she sees me as a threat, and you're well aware of that. You lied about why you took so long collecting me from El Paraiso. Why did you do that if you've nothing to hide?'

His smile widened, if that was possible. 'And there was I thinking you were some little innocent, shielded from the world and its devious ways with an expensive education. You're as sharp as a tack and just as lethal if hammered in the wrong place.'

Miranda raised a dark brow at that. 'Well, you've hit the nail on the head,' she drawled cynically. 'So now we both know where we stand.'

'Here on a sun-drenched beach, out of sight of the world and its watchers.' With that his mouth came to hers. In spite of the suggestive conversation whiplashing between them, leading to this inevitable kiss, it shocked the life from Miranda's body.

She took the assault of his lips on hers, too surprised to protest, too fired by its heat and purpose to do anything but succumb to it. It deepened, quickened into something neither of them was prepared for. Louis's hand slid from the comparative safety of her naked shoulder and sped to her breast, his caress no longer one he was in control of.

The thin cotton was no barrier to the feeling and urgency of his fingers on her hardened nipples. She fell against him, weak and utterly suppliant in his arms. His mouth tore from hers with a gravelled moan that vibrated through her, nestled at her throat and drew deeply on her flesh. His hands moved to her hips, drawing her into his muscular arousal.

Miranda gasped at the intensity of the desire that trembled her body against his, wanting him to stop but powerless to utter the words. She saw the dangers for herself then, recognised the power he had over her, the unmitigated sexual power that was as remote from deep, caring, loving feelings as animals mating.

'Don't!' she gasped, the feeble utterance a contradiction of what was happening inside her. She grasped at his hair as his hands moved her skirt up, caressing the backs of her bare thighs, heating a fiery path to more intimate regions. His hands were relentless in their arousal, his mouth moved back to hers, and her lips were already parted to take him.

Her fingers tightened in his hair, wanting to hurt and yet not wanting to punish. A muddled mixture of emotions she couldn't fight or even understand.

'Miranda,' he husked deeply, suddenly forcing their bodies apart with such ferocity that she lurched back against the harsh rock.

He held her shoulders, his fingers biting into her inflamed flesh. His eyes were so dark and impenetrable that she was afraid then, more afraid of his rejection than his assault on her. His breathing was ragged, fighting for control. 'This is impossible. It has to stop,' he bit out.

'I—I know,' she croaked, fighting for her breath and her sensibility. She clutched at the shoulders of her dress—a wasted attempt at propriety after what had nearly happened. Her throat was so restricted she could hardly utter the words that needed to be spoken. 'Louis,' she gasped. His pupils dilated as he watched her mouth move. 'It's Catherine, isn't it?'

She had known, since the minute the lovely blonde had confronted them on the veranda, known that she was a special person in his life. Why else would she be there? And why else would Mendoza try to warn her off? They both knew the power of their attraction to each other; it was here, now, still crackling between them like live electrodes. But also between them was Catherine, sparking a warning to the two of them.

'Yes, it's Catherine.' His admission came like a torrent of molten lava. 'We are engaged to be married.'

CHAPTER FOUR

MIRANDA didn't know why she hadn't foreseen that. Lovers she had been almost prepared for, but marriage was a commitment that indeed spelled danger.

'Oh, I ... didn't ...' Her voice vaporised into the hot air.

'You didn't expect that,' Louis finished for her. His body had slackened as if getting that off his chest had solved all his problems. Of course, it had. Now she knew.

'How could you do that?' she breathed at last. 'How could you make love to me when...when...?'

'When I'm engaged to be married to another woman?' He frowned, darkly, his face drawn. 'For a start, we never made it, Miranda, and we won't, though the temptation is there.'

'And what if the temptation presents itself again?' she ventured to ask, the shock of the knowledge that he was about to be married scorning all decency from her. The right thing to do was walk away, let things be, but she wanted to know, was desperate to know why a man in love with one woman could practically seduce another he barely knew.

'It won't,' he stated with such flat assurance that Miranda let out a small cry of derisory protest. 'No, it won't!' he emphasised. 'And I'll tell you why—because you aren't going to allow it.'

'So it's up to me, is it? Are you appealing to my sense of decency when it's obvious you're sadly lacking in that direction?' she blurted furiously.

'I know the difference between right and wrong and that's why we are standing here arguing instead of thrashing around in the sand at this moment!' He was angry now, with himself as well as her. A fury that only served to spur Miranda on.

'A kiss and a fumble is as deep a betrayal as the complete sexual act. Doesn't that bother your twisted conscience?'

'It troubles me as much it must trouble you.'

'Huh! My conscience is clear. I'm not engaged to anyone any more.'

'What you're saying is that you'd go ahead knowing that Catherine is my wife-to-be, and is at this moment just over there——' he nodded his head in the direction of the villa '—organising a welcome dinner for you tonight!'

'Oh, no, you don't, Mendoza!' Miranda shot fire at him. 'Don't try and twist what I say and don't try and lay blame for what has happened on my doorstep, and don't try to make me feel guilty. You tried to seduce me knowing you have a deep commitment to another woman, I let you because I was ignorant of that fact. If I had known, it wouldn't have happened!'

'That's exactly what I wanted to hear from you. Now you know and that's why it won't happen again...'

'You bet it won't!' she stormed. 'But I'd still like to hear your pathetic little excuse for your disgusting conduct!'

'There's no excuse whatsoever. You were a temptation I very nearly succumbed to. I'm not proud of it but at least I've admitted it. I hope that's enough for you.'

'Not nearly enough, you selfish bastard! Go ahead, run rings round my emotions, then put the knife in——'

'Miranda, that's enough!' he blazed, stepping towards her so violently that she thought he was going to hit her. His body shuddered as he controlled himself. 'Fighting like this doesn't help. I understand how you feel——'

'You don't,' she interrupted him coldly. 'I suppose you think your masculinity is your excuse? It's all right for men to act that way—almost expected of them—but let me tell you women's hormones function differently. Yours are on automatic pilot, ours need handling with gentle loving care. I would have thought that being engaged to darling Catherine would have taught you that? Or maybe that's the problem; maybe she hasn't enough precious hormones to keep up with your insatiable appetite!'

She didn't wait for a reply to that, sensing his anger was not quite as controlled as it might be. She swung round in the sand and headed determinedly for the villa, her lips set mutinously and her heart pounding so furiously she thought it would burst.

She didn't need all this—all this emotional turmoil. She was determinedly calm by the time she got back to the villa, though hesitant as to what to do. She had no money; how could she get off this island without it?

She ran into Sunset on the veranda as she leapt up the steps from the lawn. The girl was carrying a covered tray.

'Miss Miranda, you've had no lunch. Naomi made up a tray for you.'

Food. She didn't want to eat but her stomach told her otherwise. She'd had nothing but coffee all day, nothing substantial since the soup Mendoza had made for her last night.

'Thank you, Sunset. That was thoughtful of her.' It struck her that it had been noted she hadn't eaten lunch. Were the whole staff instructed to keep a watchful eye on her? Watch in case she ran off with the family silver?

She sat down at the cane table outside her bedroom and thought about her uncle who had landed her in this awful situation. She was becoming obsessed with his guilt and if she was to make something of her future it must stop. But how could it, with attitudes like Catherine's to cope with? Catherine. Mendoza's bride-to-be. Why, oh, why was that more difficult to cope with than anything else?

Sunset placed the tray down on the table in front of her and watched Miranda warily as the latter slowly forked prawns from a dish of mixed seafood.

'Don't you like it here, Miss Miranda?'

The question was such a surprise that Miranda didn't know what to say. She swallowed hard. 'W-why do you ask?'

'You don't look happy, and...and your new clothes were all over the floor. Don't...don't you like them?' Sunset stood back against the veranda, waiting for her reply. Her huge eyes wide, like a child who didn't understand.

Miranda felt guilty then. The plaintive look in Sunset's eyes indicated she somehow felt it was her fault Miranda wasn't happy.

'They didn't fit. I was cross because they didn't fit.'

A wide grin lit Sunset's face. 'Mr Mendoza bought them for you. Men don't understand. I'll alter them for you if you want me to.'

'That won't be necessary, Sunset. I have my pareus.' She started to eat the side-dish of salad, which was deliciously fresh and crisp.

'Pareus are for the beach, Miss Miranda.' Sunset shifted uneasily as if she shouldn't have given such an opinion. 'And besides,' she went on hurriedly, trying to exonerate herself but unwittingly condemning Catherine in the process, 'Miss Catherine told me to throw them away.'

'She did what?' Miranda's retort was so explosive that Sunset flinched.

For Sunset's sake Miranda hung on to her temper. It wasn't the poor girl's fault. At that moment Louis Mendoza strode along the veranda.

'You can go now, Sunset,' he said. 'On behalf of Miss Miranda thank Naomi for her lunch.' He sat down at the other chair across the table and helped himself to a glass of lime juice from the jug on the tray.

When Sunset was out of earshot, Miranda spoke. 'You didn't have to show me up in front of the staff; I've already thanked Sunset for the lunch.'

'So you do know how to behave after all,' he cut back.

'Yes, but it's a pity Catherine doesn't.'

'What's that supposed to mean? You're not trying to cause trouble already, are you?'

Miranda refused to rise to that. 'She ordered Sunset to throw away my pareus. Without consulting me. They were my clothes and she had no right to dispose of them.'

'I agree,' he said to her surprise. 'I'll have a word with her.'

'That's not necessary. I'm perfectly capable of fighting my own battles, thank you. I do have a mouth in my head.'

'Yes, and you'd be wise to use it sensibly.'

'Don't tell me what I can say and what I can't!' Miranda grated, trying so very hard to keep cool when all she wanted to do was get her hands round Catherine's throat and choke the last breath from her body.

'I don't want any trouble between the two of you,' he said quietly. 'So cool it, Miranda. The island is small and minor upsets can quickly explode into something bigger. This is a peaceful house and everything runs smoothly.'

'Tell Catherine that! I've done and said nothing to upset anyone yet. It's she who's causing the aggravation, insulting me behind my back, taking it upon herself to dictate what I wear.' Sulkily Miranda speared a tomato and thrust it in her mouth.

'You're right and I've told you I'll have a word with her, and that will be that, no more problems. Now let's forget all this and get down to something more constructive than a bundle of faded pareus!'

His voice was so forceful, and Miranda let the tomato slide down her throat with the help of a gulp. OK, she'd let this niggling grievance go; for the sake of a quiet life she'd swallow her pride this time, but just let something else happen, one word out of place and she'd let rip—Mendoza's fiancée or not!

'We need to talk about your future,' Louis went on, relaxing slightly and leaning back in the chair. 'Have you any idea what you want to do?'

'Apart from fading out of your life as soon as possible, you mean?'

'Cut the sarcasm, Miranda, and show a bit of that fine education you've been privileged with.'

'The diplomas for etiquette, eloquence and ecology, you mean?'

'I said cut the sarcasm and I mean it!'

She was delighted at how easily she could irritate him. It was almost worth being here just to arouse his anger and watch him writhing to control it.

'I wasn't being sarcastic, actually. It's the truth. The three "E"s. It was that sort of education.' She carried on eating. Let him pick the bones out of that!

To her chagrin he smiled, that smile that lit his face and sent her heart drumming.

'Sounds to me the perfect combination for what I have in mind for you.'

'Oh, yes, what's that? Organising cocktail parties for Greenpeace?'

He stood up, the smile gone, his body so tensed she could almost hear the thrum of his muscles tautening.

'I'll talk to you in a hundred years, when you've got rid of that chip off your shoulder!' He walked away and Miranda stood up, suddenly sorry for her childish behaviour.

'Mendoza,' she called softly. He turned. 'I'm sorry,' she murmured plaintively.

'Are you?' His brow rose like twin serpents over cold eyes. 'I doubt that.' He walked away and though Miranda called out once more he ignored her.

Why was she doing this? she asked herself later as she headed for the pool for a swim before siesta. She was making everything so much worse for herself yet she couldn't stop stabbing at him.

She slipped off her robe, one of Mendoza's purchases that didn't matter that it was several sizes too big, and dived into the pool in her own bikini. That and the shells were the only possessions left to her.

She swam several lengths, strongly and powerfully, then hauled herself out and lay on one of the loungers by the pool to dry off before going back to her room to rest in the heat of the afternoon.

She didn't rest when she got back to her room, though. She'd been thinking about her uncle. She found writing paper and pens in the top drawer of her dressing-table, and make-up, too. Mendoza had thought of everything. It stabbed at her conscience. He was doing his best and her uncle was doing what he thought best for her, too. Now was the time to back down and try not to be such a bitch.

She wrote a long letter to her uncle, hoping he was well and telling him how she was, and telling him how perfect everything was on San Paola. As she sealed the envelope she reflected on that. Perfection. Louis Mendoza was probably the most perfect specimen of a man she had ever met, physically, that was. His macho arrogance was something else, though. He was a snake where his treatment of women was concerned. Miranda knew she could never be a friend of Catherine's but it didn't stop her feeling sorry for her. Marriage to him would be like living with an unpredictable anaconda, not knowing when it was going to swallow you whole and squeeze the life-blood from you. She wondered how long the marriage would last.

'Oh, Sunset! It's perfect, just perfect.'

Miranda twirled in front of the mirror, her eyes bright with pleasure. The cool, lemony chiffon creation fitted like a second skin to the upper part of her body and swirled sensually over her hips and flared out around her long slender legs. It had tiny sleeves that just covered the graze on her shoulder and was cut low down her bronzed back. The front was a dream of simplicity, the edge of the fabric rolled finely around the neckline.

'It's very sexy,' Sunset smiled.

'Is it?' Miranda laughed, knowing full well it was. 'Thank you, Sunset.' The girl beamed her pleasure. 'You've worked so hard on it. I didn't expect it. A wonderful surprise. But why this one?'

'Because tonight is special. Your first night with us.'

Sunset had altered the one dress she would have chosen to wear herself if it had fitted. Now it did, perfectly. She slipped on delicate yellow strappy sandals with narrow high heels and looked at herself in the mirror.

If it weren't for the dramatic loss of weight and the deep brown of her tan she might have been the Miami socialite she'd left behind in her past. The temptation to fling off the dress in favour of something less sophisticated was overthrown by the pleasure she felt at the silkiness of the fabric next to her skin. She'd always liked nice clothes. Her rebellion at casting them out of her life after the trial was beginning to look like a childish theatrical tantrum. She sighed. Yesterday she hadn't wanted to exchange her desolate island life, today she was already seduced back to civilisation with a sexy chiffon dress. She had no choice but to go along with it now.

'Just one more thing,' Sunset cried with excitement. She ran from the bedroom and Miranda sat down at the dressing-table. She stared down at the assortment of make-up Mendoza had bought for her. Every combination of shades was there, as he couldn't have known her colouring; he'd never set eyes on her before El Paraiso.

Carefully she selected a lipstick, some pale eyeshadow and a black mascara to tint the edges of her sun-bleached lashes and got to work.

Sunset burst back into the room with a handful of pale apricot-coloured hibiscus flowers. With breathless excitement she scooped Miranda's raven hair to one side and clipped the flowers in place behind her ear.

'There, now you look as if you belong to the island,' she laughed.

It was all the added adornment Miranda needed. Somehow a compromise, no jewellery from her past life, just island flowers.

Sunset insisted on introducing Miranda to the housekeeper, Naomi, before taking her through to the sitting-room for pre-dinner drinks with Catherine and Louis.

Naomi was in the huge air-conditioned kitchen putting the finishing touches to chicken in lime sauce.

'Oh, Miss Miranda. Sure good to meet you at last. Sunset has told me all about you.'

She was a huge lady, with that odd balletic grace so common to very large ladies. She rolled towards Miranda and gave her such a hug it knocked the breath from her. She laughed all the time, an infectious laugh that jostled her whole body. As with Sunset, Miranda liked her on sight.

'Now, be off with you to the sitting-room or you'll vex Miss Catherine. That one is hot on punctuality,' she gurgled.

Sunset escorted Miranda along the veranda to the sitting-room; the patio doors were wide open, as was every door and window in the villa. Sunset touched Miranda's arm lightly, sensing Miranda's sudden nervousness, a small gesture that went straight to Miranda's heart. If all was hell around her she guessed she had two friends in Sunset and Naomi.

Miranda stepped into the doorway, pausing to take in her surroundings. She'd explored the grounds but not the villa and this bright, spacious room wasn't a disappointment. Glass and cool designer chrome, champagne-coloured leather and lush green potted ferns.

Catherine was draped on the sofa in ice-blue silk to match her eyes, her mouth gaping open at the sight of Miranda, very unladylike. She quickly contorted her lips into a grimace of a smile.

'How lovely to see you, Miranda, and looking so... so rested.'

'Hardly the description I would afford her,' Louis said, coming towards her. 'You look lovely, Miranda.' He bent and brushed a kiss against her cheek, then whipped the compliment away from her by adding, 'Glad to see you are coming to your senses at last.'

'Yes, Miranda,' Catherine cut in quickly, too quickly. She hadn't liked that small show of affection from her fiancé. 'You look quite normal now.'

A hundred intrepid retorts spurred to Miranda's lips and by some small miracle she managed to curb the lot of them. That kiss had helped, stunned her with its daring. In that swift, unexpected contact she had experienced a galaxy of sensations. Warmth, softness, the headiness of some exclusive cologne and one that shone above the others like the Dogstar Sirius—sensuality. It hit her in the solar plexus.

'A drink, Miranda?' Louis offered.

'Just a tonic water, thank you.' She smiled and sat down, perching herself tensely on the edge of one of the soft leather armchairs.

'That's Louis's chair...'

'Catherine!' warned Louis, without turning his attention away from the bar at the far end of the cool room. 'Don't be pernickety.'

Pernickety! Why, the atmosphere dripped pure venom! So the happy couple weren't so very happy tonight. She couldn't be the cause, surely? Mendoza might be a snake but he wouldn't be so cruel as to give Catherine any idea of what had happened down on the beach this afternoon.

'You might sense an atmosphere, Miranda,' Louis smoothed as he handed her a bubbling tonic water, ice tinkling against the crystal. 'It's the time of the year. The rainy season is approaching and Catherine is getting edgy.'

'So would you if you suffered the migraines I do,' Catherine murmured. 'If you must know, Miranda...' Miranda hadn't insisted on knowing anything! '...I'm trying to persuade Louis to come back to Florida with me for a couple of months; it's hell here from September, the rain and humidity unbearable——'

'I'm sure Miranda doesn't want to hear how unbearable you find it,' Louis interjected.

'On the contrary, Miranda ought to know just how ghastly it is. If she's going to be here for a year——'

'I've spent time in the Caribbean before,' Miranda interrupted firmly. 'I'm used to the climate and I don't suffer from migraines.'

'Lucky you; all the same I think Louis is being totally selfish in not coming back with me. Being apart will be just too much of a drag. Don't you agree, Miranda?'

'That Mendoza is selfish or being apart too much of a drag?' It was the best Miranda could do. It raised a glimmer of a smile at the corner of Louis's mouth.

Catherine's mouth pouted. 'Well, both, if you put it like that.'

'Not knowing either of you well enough, I wouldn't want to side with either of you,' Miranda offered and then she did a mysterious and dangerous thing and found herself siding with Louis. 'I'm sure Mendoza has reasons for not wanting to leave the island for so long, so why don't you stay if you are so desperate not to be apart? I'm sure there are some wonderful medications for migraine on the market!'

There was a small gasp from Catherine and a laugh from Louis. Miranda's eyes flicked from one to the other like windscreen-wipers in a tropical storm, which was precisely what this was brewing up into.

'I think Miranda should know the truth—that you don't want to miss the social season in Florida.' Louis stood between the two of them, and directed his words to Miranda. 'Her fine-weather friends scuttle from the islands when the rains come. Poor Catherine here will be without her companions for a few months. They all migrate back to Florida like rare exotic flamingoes, take up their dry martinis and quaff on relentlessly.'

If Miranda had been Catherine she would have got up and swamped Mendoza with the very derisive martini she had clutched in her hand. To her utter amazement Catherine let out a light laugh that tinkled round the room and darkened Louis's brow.

'Whatever turns you on, sweetheart.' She gulped at her drink, which was a clear indication to Miranda that she was covering up her true feelings, almost as if she was afraid of her fiancé yet couldn't resist egging him on. With baited breath Miranda waited for the next onslaught, but was disappointed when Catherine turned her undivided attention to her.

'Miranda, dear. Why do you insist on addressing Louis as Mendoza? I'm sure it irritates the hell out of him.'

Miranda held her fury in check. She was being used here, part of their painful cut-and-thrust game.

'I don't know,' she admitted, turning her eyes to Louis. 'A bad habit I've got into, I suppose.'

Louis drained his drink, glanced at his watch. 'I do believe you called me by my Christian name once. I wonder why it was only the once? Perhaps I should put that to rights.' He locked his dark eyes into hers, a look that Catherine couldn't witness because she was out of eye contact with him.

Heated blood rushed to Miranda's face at that painful reminder. Yes, she'd uttered his Christian name, an impassioned plea as he'd tried to make love to her, and did he mean that threat to tempt her to use it again? She knew in that awful moment that he did. Some time, somewhere he'd take her in his arms again and force his name from her lips.

'It's not for you to put to rights, Louis. It's all down to me, as I recall you once said.' Miranda gave him a forced smile, subtly reminding him of the earlier conversation down on the beach. She shrugged her shoulders. 'You see, it's quite easy when I try. You're glancing at your watch, Louis.' She laid emphasis on his name and he smiled a *touché*. 'Does that mean it's time to eat? I'm starving.' She beamed then, a genuine smile of pleasure.

'How dared you, how dared you do that to me?' Miranda blazed later.

Catherine's threatened migraine had arrived prematurely, several weeks early, in fact, and she had retired to bed after the coffee and brandy.

Miranda and Louis were alone, sitting outside on the veranda. Miranda was feeling decidedly sick—a combination of unaccustomed rich food and a surfeit of wicked innuendoes flung between the engaged couple.

'Am I supposed to know what you are talking about?' Louis drawled, his eyes not moving from the seascape spread out beyond the veranda.

'You know exactly what I'm talking about. You're just trying to be difficult. Tonight you two talked round me, over me and under me. You were both playing some sort of vicious game with each other and I felt like a worn-out tennis ball slamming between the pair of you! Is that how you treat your guests?'

'You're not a guest but part of the family now.'

'And that was the welcome party, was it?' Miranda sneered.

'I'm sorry if it upset you, but that's the way we are.'

'Great! I'd say the bluebird of happiness will sing every day of your married life!' she grated sarcastically. She frowned, not understanding the perplexities of such a sabre-edged relationship. 'Is it always like that?'

'Only when Catherine doesn't get her own way, which seems to be most of the time lately,' he admitted on a sigh. 'We have our moments, though.'

'And have you had one of those moments since you brought me here?' A daring question she was spurred to ask because of the horror of the whole evening.

He turned and looked at her then. 'What sort of question is that?'

'I would have thought you know me well enough by now to read that one.' He offered not a word so Miranda crashed on. 'In plain English, then, have you made love to her since we arrived?'

His smile was more of a sneer. 'What a voyeuristic curiosity you have! Does that sort of thing turn you on?'

'The thought fascinates me,' Miranda said, refusing to be insulted or side-tracked. 'You can't keep your hands off me, so I presume you have a high libido; Catherine is as tightly strung as an over-tuned cello and you are hardly Mr Cool tonight...'

'And sex is supposed to be the panacea that cures all, is it?'

'I wouldn't know,' she said mock innocently.

'Would you like to?' he drawled suggestively, holding her gaze till she gave a hoot of laughter to cover her embarrassment.

'No, you don't, Mendoza. You're twisting again. That tongue of yours is as slippery as an oil slick.'

'So it's fair game to pick over my love-life but a no goal where yours is concerned?'

'I don't have a love-life and, besides, yours is so much more interesting,' she said sweetly.

'Would it interest you to know, then, that because of you I find myself in the unique position of not wanting to make love to my fiancée?'

Miranda found it very interesting indeed, though a thousand wild horses wouldn't drag that admission from her. Tilting her chin defiantly, she smiled wickedly. 'My heart bleeds for your impotency.'

He smiled back. 'No more than mine, sweetheart, no more than mine.'

There was nothing more to be said, a state that left Miranda with an odd frustration biting at her throat. He parried her curiosity with skill, gave no more than he wanted to give. He'd admitted he was going to marry Catherine and that was all. When she probed, he parried. Very unsatisfactory indeed.

Miranda stood up. 'I'm going to bed now. Goodnight, Mendoza.'

He raised his dark head and looked at her. 'What happened to the "Louis"?'

'Old habits die hard,' she retorted.

'And can be broken with gentle persuasion or brute force, whatever turns you on.'

'Neither, Louis,' she smarmed. 'No contest!'

He held her defiant gaze long enough to set her nerve-ends jangling. And then he smiled, a self-assured smile of someone who knew he held all the winning cards in his hand. Names weren't an issue here or old habits or even games that people played. That smile was sublimely confident in the dangerous challenge he was tempting her with. Without having the last word he had nevertheless come out the victor.

Her first impulse was to strike the triumphant smile from his face, the second was to quell the fever of excitement that pulsed deep inside her. She executed neither, turned on her heel and left him with his dangerous thoughts.

CHAPTER FIVE

'LOUIS has plans for you this morning,' Catherine said at breakfast by the pool the next morning.

Miranda couldn't see Catherine's eyes behind their dark glasses to gauge what she thought of that; her voice certainly gave no indication of dissent. Boredom more than anything.

'What sort of plans?' Miranda murmured, buttering a slice of warm toast. She certainly wasn't ready to hit the social scene yet, and Catherine had made it clear that she wasn't keen to act as chaperon.

Catherine shrugged her pale shoulders under the shade of a palm-frond umbrella. 'He didn't say anything for sure but I got the impression he wants to put you to work.'

Work. It suddenly occurred to Miranda that she knew nothing of what Louis did for a living. So involved with her own predicament that she'd shown no interest.

'What does Louis do for a living?' she asked.

Catherine sipped her orange juice before replying. 'Louis is so well stashed he need never work again, but for some reason he just goes on and on.'

'On and on with what?' Miranda asked. She was irritated that Catherine was incapable or perhaps

unwilling to give her a straight answer, a bit like
Louis himself.

That annoying shrug of uninterest again from
Catherine. 'Something with yachts and property
and finance, I believe.'

'An entrepreneur?'

'Yes, that as well, I guess,' Catherine murmured,
shifting her sunglasses to the top of her head,
Florida-style.

Miranda doubted she knew what the word meant.
Or did she have other things on her mind? Her eyes
were red this morning and Miranda wondered if
her migraine attack was genuine. She certainly
didn't look too well, as if she'd spent a restless
night. Maybe she had, maybe Louis had——

'Good morning, Miranda.'

Miranda turned her head and looked up at Louis.
No, he wasn't Mr Cool this morning. He too looked
as if he'd spent a restless night, but not with the
migrained Catherine.

'Good morning, Louis,' she responded, using his
Christian name to remind him to forget last night.
'Catherine says you have plans for me this morning.
I'm pleased; a girl could die of boredom here,' she
said pointedly, giving a measured glance at
Catherine, whose attention was fully occupied with
a chipped fingernail.

'Well, when you've finished breakfast, perhaps
you would join me in the study.' He'd obviously
already taken breakfast as he didn't sit down. He
turned his attention to Catherine. 'And what are
you doing with yourself this morning?'

'Making excuses for you, as usual,' she bit back without looking at him. 'You promised to attend Margarita's charity coffee morning in aid of the boys' club.'

'I've already donated a hunk of land for a cricket pitch and the pavilion; that's as far as my charity goes, Catherine.'

Catherine pouted her annoyance but said nothing. Louis bent and planted a conciliatory kiss on her cheek, a gesture that left Catherine unmoved and Miranda surprised. 'I'll see you later, darling,' he murmured and turned away to the villa.

Catherine flicked her sunglasses back over her eyes but not before Miranda had seen the deep pain in them. It was more than disappointment that Louis was not joining her; it was a hopelessness. Miranda wished she hadn't seen it. It made her feel even more uncomfortable than last night's cut-and-thrust antics had. She swallowed the last of her toast and coffee before getting up to leave.

'I'll see you later, Catherine. Perhaps we could have a game of tennis. I haven't played for ages.' Somehow she felt she ought to try and get on with Catherine; a game of tennis might help alleviate the disparity between them.

'Well, I haven't played ever! See no point in thrashing around in this heat,' she clipped coldly. Then she turned and looked up at Miranda. 'Why don't you ask Louis to play with you? I'm sure after the deal he struck with your bent uncle you could get away with asking the earth from him.' She smiled, frostily not warmly. 'Keep that in mind,

Miranda dear. You're here under sufferance, part of a package deal. Whatever he does and says to you is because of that deal and don't you forget it.'

Miranda swung away. Not a biting retort to that bare-boned warning to call her own. Which was as well under the circumstances. Catherine already resented her presence, saw her as a threat on Louis's time, and to get into a slanging match with her would be asking for trouble. So she had no choice but to button her lip and keep a hold on herself.

Miranda found the study after barging into several bedrooms and apologising to the army of maids who kept the sprawling villa in sparkling form. All the rooms opened off from a marble-floored reception-hall at the front of the villa and had further doors to the veranda on the beach side. All except the study, which was tucked away at the side with its own small patio area overlooking the rose garden. It had seclusion and coolness and a calmness needed for its purpose.

Louis wasn't in the study and Miranda browsed. There was a multitude of books lining one wall, traditional study-type furniture, mahogany desk and leather chairs, photographs of yachts enlarged and framed on other walls. There was a computer, fax, photocopier, nothing very extraordinary, even though it was all set in a white villa on a small island in the Caribbean, which Miranda supposed was a bit extraordinary. If he was so successful, why wasn't he operating somewhere where the pulse beat? Miami or the Bahamas?

'Good, you're here.'

Louis came in from the patio, looking cool in white trousers and pale grey T-shirt. 'I hope you feel settled enough to want to get on with something constructive?' He sat at his desk and opened a weighty file in front of him. 'Sit down.'

Miranda flopped into a chair on the other side of the desk.

'No, not there. Here, next to me.'

With a huff Miranda shifted from one chair to another. She was here under sufferance, as Catherine had so eloquently reminded her, so whatever Louis had in mind for her was sure to be a bore.

'And don't huff like that, as if I've asked you to perform the twelve labours of Hercules,' he said, his eyes narrowing.

'Well, I hardly have Hercules's choice, do I?' She smiled cynically at him. 'Toil and duty chosen in preference to ease and pleasure.'

He raised a questioning brow. 'Is that what you want, a life of ease and pleasure?'

'Not at all, but I would like a choice in how my life progresses from here,' she told him flatly.

'Well, I'm afraid you haven't. Sadly you have to do as I say.' He paused. 'Unless of course you'd rather join Catherine on her parochial charity circuit?'

'Don't they say charity begins at home? A bit of charity on your part wouldn't go ungratified,' Miranda iced. 'I'm sure Catherine is doing her best and you seem adamant in putting her down all the time.' Why in heaven she was defending the pouting Catherine she didn't know!

'If I thought Catherine's interest lay in the needy I'd say you had a point. Unfortunately she enjoys the gossip and being seen with the right people rather than the nitty-gritty of giving aid where it's needed.'

Miranda was nearly on the point of sussing that out for herself. She'd seen it enough times in her uncle's wealthy circles. What really puzzled her was what a man like Louis Mendoza saw in the Catherine de Vaux of the world.

'You don't even love her, do you?' she challenged, wondering why she was bothering to worry this particular bone. What they did with their lives was none of her business.

Louis appeared to endorse her thoughts with a dismissive shake of his shoulders. 'We are here to discuss your future, not mine and Catherine's.'

Dead end once again. Miranda turned her attention to the file he thrust in front of her.

'What's all this? If you expect me to type all this out for you, think again. My sort aren't expected to earn their keep in such menial clerical tasks. In other words I was never taught to type.'

He leaned back in his chair and studied her, a fraction of a grin warming his face. 'And what are beautiful ladies of your sort expected to do with their lives?'

Miranda back-handed the 'beautiful' compliment to the recesses of her mind. 'We are expected to marry well.' It was a sad fact of life. 'After my education in Europe my uncle threw me into New York society life to trawl for a husband worthy of the money he'd splashed out on me.'

'And came up with this Presler of yours?'

Miranda shook her head and smiled. 'A New York lawyer? Not good enough for Sagan Gordon. He dangled me in front of a greasy shipping magnate old enough to be my father...'

'And you turned tail and dived headlong into the arms of the first man that caught your eye.'

'Something like that.' Miranda could actually smile at the memory of Presler now. 'I did pitch for him. He was very handsome, young and ambitious. Not much of a catch, I realise now. Ironic, but my uncle got his own way in the end—but not in the way he intended. He hated Presler.'

'And if it weren't for the guilty verdict on your uncle you would have married him?'

'Yes, and lived happily ever after, the way you and Catherine are going to.' She couldn't resist that sarcastic gibe.

Louis took it on the chin. 'Now I see why Sagan steered you into my care—to save you from yourself. With your misguided sense of injustice you could end up marrying a parking-lot attendant.'

Miranda held his eyes. 'If I loved him enough it wouldn't matter what he did for a living.' She said it with such conviction that he believed her.

'Lucky man,' he muttered, and flicked through the papers in his file. 'Now, let's leave the bleeding hearts out of this and get on.'

Miranda got the impression he was suddenly filled with anger, but put that behind her. Now wasn't the time to wonder why.

Just for the hell of it she'd planned on stifling a yawn of boredom as he started to outline what he thought might interest her—the projected plan for his intentions for the four islands he'd purchased from her uncle. But to her surprise it caught her imagination. Probably because she was familiar with them—a clever move on Louis's part.

'Your uncle used the islands for his fishing trips and I see no reason not to expand on that. The Americans come down to the Caribbean in droves to pursue deep-sea fishing. We can lodge them on the islands and take them out from there.'

Miranda picked up the plans for the high-class chalets he was thinking of constructing on three of those islands, El Paraiso not being one of them. Miranda asked why.

'Simply because of its inaccessibility. I can build marinas on the others but I'd have to destroy the coral reefs around El Paraiso to get access and I don't want to do that.'

Miranda admired him for that. 'So El Paraiso is a no goer?'

He shrugged. 'I had to take the chaff with the wheat. Three out of four isn't so bad.'

Miranda liked the thought of the lovely island being left unspoiled by crowds of fish-hungry hunters from the States. But there was something Louis had overlooked.

She shifted the map of the islands in front of them. 'You'll lose the coral reefs anyway,' she told him quietly.

Louis frowned and bent over the map. 'How do you mean?'

Miranda stabbed at the island closest to El Paraiso with the tip of her finger. 'This is your biggest planned construction. Thirty chalets with a bar and restaurant, so you're going to get quite a crowd, all within striking distance of an untouched island. Taking human nature for what it is, it won't be untouched for long. Some smart alec will want to get there just because it's there. And you know what tourists are like for souvenirs: they'll strip those coral beds in a blink of an eye.'

Louis leaned back and chewed at his pen. 'I don't see how I can avoid that.'

Miranda laughed at his lack of foresight. It was obvious he hadn't dabbled in anything like this before. Nor had she, come to that; but he was supposed to be the entrepreneur.

'Develop them,' she suggested. 'Everyone else conservation-conscious is doing it, developing underwater gardens. Then you educate people to enjoy the reefs and go home happy with a photograph or two of live coral instead of a chunk of the real thing. Trips with a qualified instructor can be organised from the main island, glass-bottomed boats, underwater cameras, scuba equipment. The hardy can swim ashore if they want to and at the end of the day you ship them back to where they

PLAY THE

LUCKY CARNIVAL WHEEL

and get as many as

SIX FREE GIFTS...

FREE! THIS CUDDLY TEDDY BEAR!

You'll love this little teddy bear. He's soft and cuddly with an adorable expression that's sure to make you smile.

PLAY THE LUCKY "CARNIVAL WHEEL"

Scratch away the silver panel. Then look for your number below to see which gifts you're entitled to!

YES! Please send me all the free books and gifts to which I am entitled. I understand that I am under no obligation to purchase anything ever. If I choose to subscribe to the Mills & Boon Reader Service I will receive 6 brand new Romances for just £9.60 every month. There is no charge for postage and packing. I may cancel or suspend my subscription at anytime simply by writing to you. The free books and gifts are mine to keep in anycase. I am over 18 years of age.

MS/MRS/MISS/MR _____

ADDRESS _____

_____ POSTCODE _____

SIGNATURE _____

3A2R

41	WORTH 4 FREE BOOKS, A FREE CUDDLY TEDDY AND FREE MYSTERY GIFT.
29	WORTH 4 FREE BOOKS, AND A FREE CUDDLY TEDDY.
17	WORTH 4 FREE BOOKS.
5	WORTH 2 FREE BOOKS.

ASSOCIATION OF MAIL ORDER PUBLISHERS

mps MAILING PREFERENCE SERVICE

POST THIS CARD TODAY!

Mills & Boon Reader Service
FREEPOST
P.O. Box 236
Croydon
Surrey
CR9 9EL

POST THIS CARD TODAY!

NO
STAMP
NEEDED

can't do any harm. That way everyone will be happy.'

There was such a long-protracted silence after her enthusiastic outburst that Miranda wondered if she had made a fool of herself. She let out a sigh. 'Sorry. I got a bit carried away.'

Louis said nothing, gathered all the papers together and slid them back into the file. Well, she had thought it a good idea if he hadn't. So much for her efforts. Perhaps she ought to learn to type after all.

'Would you like to see round the island?' he asked unexpectedly.

'Yes, very much. I'd like to change into shorts first, though; I'm too hot in this dress.' She was melting and shorts would be far more comfortable in a car.

'I'll meet you out the front in twenty minutes. I have a few phone calls to make.' He picked up the phone before she had left the room, his brow darkened in concentration.

Miranda was glad to be out of the study and into fresh air. She could imagine what was going through his mind, the regrets for ever involving himself with her for a year. Of course she'd made a fool of herself with her ideas for the coral reefs; she should have kept quiet. So now he knew just how useless she was. She wondered what he would come up with next to occupy her.

'That's your car, by the way,' Louis told her as she joined him later after changing into a pair of khaki shorts Sunset had altered for her, not too tight for comfort, and a baggy vest-top T-shirt. Miranda was cool and at ease, till Louis waved his hand at the sleek white convertible in the bank of open-fronted garages to the side of the pink drive. Her stomach tensed. She hadn't expected such a decent-looking car.

'Who have I to thank for that—you or my uncle?'

She climbed into the ancient Land Rover he'd backed out of the garage.

'Your uncle, I'm afraid. He had it shipped down here for you. Obviously knows your taste in expensive cars. If I'd had my way I'd have supplied you with a Mini moke to run around in.'

'Meaning you don't think I'm worthy of a sporty BMW?' she crisped back, quite hurt by his implication.

'Meaning this island doesn't boast a slick freeway to cruise down at a hundred miles an hour, as you'll find out in a minute.'

She did, to her stomach's horror. Once out of the long palm-flanked driveway they jolted along on a road pitted with pot-holes.

'I see what you mean,' she cried, hanging on to the overhead roll-bar to brace herself.

Mercifully they soon reached an asphalt road with so many twists and turns in it that a roller-coaster would have been more suited to it. But at least now she was being thrown from side to side instead of up and down.

Miranda soon forgot her discomfort as the lovely island unfolded in front of her. It was much smaller than she had imagined. They had driven right across it in next to no time and were facing bright green sea again. Louis swung the wheel and they took the coastal road, which was quite civilised with beautiful villas dotted along the stretch of glaring white sands.

'There are surprisingly few permanent residents here. Most of those are vacation homes.' He nodded towards the villas.

'I thought you had quite a thriving community here, by the way Catherine spoke of coffee-mornings and dinner parties.'

Louis smiled. 'Yes, I suppose she gave that impression. Truth is that most of the year it does buzz here, but the rains drive them back. It's pretty quiet here then—the best time of all for me.'

That statement was quite revealing to Miranda but when she came to think of it was it so surprising? She had seen him coping with the primitive life on tiny El Paraiso with the ease of a native of the islands. It prompted her next question.

'Have you always lived here?'

'I was born in Jamaica; my father was a diplomat, my mother a doctor, and they live in Canada now. I was educated in England and America. Couldn't settle in either, though. The islands are in my blood. I have offices in Miami but I spend as little time as possible there.'

No doubt where he met Catherine, but Miranda didn't pursue it. All was going well with them; in fact Miranda was enjoying herself, to her surprise. To bring Catherine into the conversation would be asking for trouble again. They always seemed to have harsh words when she was mentioned.

Louis took her to lunch on the beach, a simple beach-bar where they ate crab backs and drank cold beer. There was quite a crowd there, locals and regular tourists, and Louis knew them all. He made a point of introducing Miranda to everyone and though Miranda steeled herself when Louis stated her name she had no need. Everyone was very friendly and welcoming and showed no sign of the animosity Catherine had hinted at.

'Perhaps they didn't realise who I was,' Miranda added after saying how nice everyone had been to her. They were on their way to a dry dock at the point of the island where Louis wanted to check on the progress of a yacht that was being built for him.

'They know exactly who you are and who your uncle is. News travels fast on a tiny island like this,' he told her.

'Yes, but Catherine...' She was about to repeat what she had overheard, but Louis bit into her words.

'Catherine isn't the island oracle and she has no right to form opinions for other people.'

'But——'

'Forget it, Miranda.' His voice was adamant and Miranda choked back her words. Louis's brow darkened as if he had the weight of the world's problems round his neck and she turned away from him to gaze at the passing scenery, mainly sugar cane at this end of the island.

Something was bothering Louis and she longed to know what. She longed to know more of his strained relationship with Catherine, too. For a couple of supposed lovers they were hardly Love's sweet dream. An arranged marriage crossed her mind, or maybe something of a lesser arrangement, a marriage of convenience. It was obvious Catherine came from good stock and Louis had proved he was not averse to a bit of wheeling and dealing in mortal souls. Funny if Catherine was part of some deal, as she was. She wondered what he might have traded for her!

She tried to show interest in the boat yard but the beer and the oppressive heat were getting to her. While Louis was in deep conversation with his men Miranda wandered around, keeping to the shade of several yacht hulls to ward off the heat of the sun.

'You look as if you could do with a swim,' he said as he came to find her. Miranda was slumped down on an upturned crate, too hot to pace another step.

She smiled up at him. 'Can't wait.'

He reached out to haul her to her feet, wrongly assessing her weight so that he nearly hauled her into his arms. Miranda's breath caught in her throat as she tried to jerk back from him. Their eyes locked, momentarily. Miranda felt a different sort of heat scorch through her, one she had been unconsciously warding off all day. Something deep inside her had programmed her through the day, repelling the closeness of him in the study, sitting next to him in the Land Rover. Now it all crackled through her, the sensations she had not wanted to heed, the heat, the smell, the look of him.

Why wouldn't it go away, the awareness of him? It hurt her, a physical pain she didn't want or need in her life. And what was spanning through his mind? she wondered as he took forever to release her hand. His eyes, surely the mirror of his soul, gave nothing away. A controlled muscle at his temple said it all, though. Hold back. After all, he was engaged to be married.

Miranda sat stiffly next to him in the Land Rover as they headed back home. Could she call it home? It had to be for a year. An impossible year. By the end of it she would probably be sharing it with Mr and Mrs Mendoza. She concentrated her thoughts on the welcoming pool back at the villa. She would swim and swim Louis Mendoza out of her system.

'Aren't we going in the wrong direction?' she ventured to ask, as they appeared to be heading inland along a narrow rough track rather than towards the coast-road that would take them back.

'Depends where you want to go,' he said nonchalantly. 'I'm heading for a swim.'

A short-cut through a tropical forest. Miranda closed her eyes. Good, the sooner they were back at the villa the better.

'Oh.' It was all she could muster as the Land Rover came to a bumpy halt in a shady clearing. It was cooler here but her pulse overheated at the seclusion that enveloped them like a dark green blanket.

'I'll show you my favourite water-hole,' he said, springing from the Land Rover.

He bestowed that upon her as if he was privileging her with some closely guarded secret. He took her hand and led her through waist-high ferns, warm and sticky to the touch. She gripped his hand tightly for fear of anything that might crawl out of their denseness, recalling the snake that had wriggled out from similar ferns on El Paraiso and had nearly sent her heart leaping out from her ribcage.

'Oh, it's beautiful!' Miranda exclaimed as the ferns thinned to reveal a blue lagoon as bright and clear as a sapphire. Silver fish flashed in the sunlight just below the surface and turtles sunned themselves on the tiny strip of sand that edged the vivid blue like a Puritan lace collar. The lagoon was fed from the sea in the distance by a long winding strip of water so narrow and overgrown as to be impassable by boat.

Miranda was struck by the stillness and the solitude. She understood why it was Louis's favourite water-hole. It was made in heaven and deposited here on earth.

She started in horror as Louis started to strip. 'I—I didn't bring anything to swim in,' she uttered quickly.

'Nor did I.' He discarded his T-shirt and went for the zipper of his trousers. He looked up at the shocked expression flaming her cheeks. He grinned. 'Don't worry. I won't embarrass you.' He let his trousers down to reveal white boxer-shorts. 'I'll swim in these.'

In fascination she watched him wade into the water, his body so athletic and tuned to perfection that she marvelled at its darkness, its power. He dived under the water, surfaced and struck out to where the blue darkened with the depth of the water. She longed to go after him, to cool her heated flesh, to match his powerful strokes and show him what a good swimmer she was. But why should she want to do that?

Miranda slumped despondently down to the sand and hugged her knees. She wanted his approval, that was why! His approval of something she could do well. So far he thought her pretty ineffectual at everything. Her enthusiastic ideas for the coral reefs had met with a stony silence indicating he thought it a crazy idea and she crazy along with it.

'Damn you!' she muttered as a trickle of moisture ran down her spine, soaking into the waistband of her already damp shorts. The temptation was too much. She stood up, careful eyes on Louis in case he turned and saw her stripping off her shorts. Her tiny briefs were red and resembled the bottom half of a bikini anyway, but she wore no bra and no way was she going to take off her T-shirt. She ran into the warm water with it intact.

Soft, warm currents of water caressed her legs as she cleaved through the water. It was deliciously sensual, a feeling she allowed to envelop her. She headed in the opposite direction to Louis, dived and discovered the underwater fantasy world of exotic fish, startled by her presence and scattering in all directions around her alien brown body. Surfacing for air, she gulped and dived again, teased a shy sea anemone with the tip of her finger, and swam towards a clump of wavering sea-grass to discover its secrets.

'Miranda the mermaid,' Louis husked as she surfaced again. She was so engrossed that she'd been unaware of him swimming towards her. 'What have you discovered down there?'

Miranda trod water, swept her hair back from her face, blinked her watery eyes.

'You startled me,' she gasped, her voice thick in her throat.

'I didn't mean to.' His hand snaked out and grasped her wrist. 'Show me what you've found.'

She blinked her eyes at him uncertainly, not understanding the force of his hand wrapped round her wrist. It was urging her down, urging her into that fantasy world below, but more than that it was daring her. To what she wasn't sure but had no time to reflect as he suddenly up-ended and disappeared below the surface of the water, dragging her down with him. She had a split second to gulp air before the water closed over her head, fanning her hair out around her.

Panic seized her. This was more than a voyage of marine discovery; it was a shared intimacy she wanted no part of. He let go of her wrist and struck out for an outcrop of rocks on the sea bed. He turned and beckoned her and the fear of him receded in a current of warm water. She followed, angry for that second of panic she had allowed herself; it had almost exhausted her air supply.

Louis hung on to a rock and raised a warning index finger at her and then pointed to a cluster of spiky black sea-urchins nestling between them. She nodded her acknowledgement, knowing the dangers of one of those poisonous spines piercing the flesh. Louis moved to another gathering of rocks, snatching at a long-vacated conch-shell trapped between them. He raised it and jerked it upwards and they both surfaced for air, gasping and filling their lungs as soon as they broke through the water.

'A present to add to your collection,' he smiled, water coursing in rivulets down his face.

Miranda's heart lurched painfully at the simple gift and the obvious pleasure it gave him to hand it to her. She took it and smiled her thanks, all words locked in her throat as the shell had been locked between the rocks.

She swam back to the shore, slowly, for now she was tired. She heard the gentle swoosh of him swimming behind her. In the shallow water she scrambled to her feet and, clutching the shell to her chest, paddled ashore.

She turned on the beach and her lips parted in a mixture of shock and an unwarranted thrill that wavered through every sinew of her lean body at the sight of him coming towards her. The silence folded round her till all she could hear was her own heartbeat, thunderous and surging with heat in her ears. She couldn't look away; it was impossible. And he knew, knew what he was doing to her.

His deeply bronzed body coursed water, straightened the tight curls on his chest, gleamed every strained muscle that rippled his body.

Unwillingly and yet uninhibited, her eyes lowered. The wet cotton of his shorts clung to him, semi-transparent and revealing, clinging to his upper thighs like a taut second skin.

She was painfully aware of her own T-shirt clinging to her breasts, her nipples surging painfully against the wet fabric, aroused by the caressing, sensual sea and more. She was heatedly aware of her own arousal, knew it and, like him, did nothing to conceal it. They watched each other as he came closer, drinking each other in, trying in desperation to slake the raging thirst and hunger inside them.

Miranda stepped back, a small cry of despair foaming on her lips. He wanted her and she wanted him and in this heaven here on earth who would know? It was another world, far removed from reality.

Part of her closed off—the good, reasoning part. She didn't want to hurt anyone, least of all herself, but the reckless, daring part of her opened up like a desert flower in the heat of the sun. Without a spoken word she was tempting him, drawing him into the power she hadn't known existed within her till now. An intangible temptation that she let flow out to him, from her eyes, her half-parted lips, her very essence.

He stood in front of her, his breath coarse and rasping, coming from somewhere deep inside him.

Miranda let the conch-shell drop to her side, didn't hear the thud of it in the deep sand. All she could hear was its hidden secret, the sea rushing in her ears, roaring wildly.

'Miranda.' He said her name roughly, regrettably, hopelessly.

She murmured what he wanted to hear in the tone he wanted to hear. 'Louis,' she urged softly.

But another screamed out from her. From the part of her that she'd closed off. The desert flower inside her flinched as the sea anemone had when she had teased it, its petals hesitant and unsure. Catherine, the sea murmured, and as Louis's mouth closed over hers the roaring in Miranda's ears swept it away with a rush of heat and liquid fire.

CHAPTER SIX

MIRANDA'S lips moved restlessly under Louis's. The joy of holding him in her arms was overwhelming. She wanted to crawl under his skin to be a part of him.

He grazed his lips from hers, lifted his hands and touched her breasts over the T-shirt clinging to her. He was watching her through heavily hooded eyes, dark and predatory, watching her face contort with the sweet rapture of his touch. Slowly he lifted the sopping fabric away from her skin. His hands worked over her flesh, gently at first then grinding into her, massaging and stimulating her till her senses spun dizzily. The ache and the need drove hard inside her, weakening her till a small cry broke from her inflamed lips.

'Do you want me to stop?' he husked roughly.

She never wanted him to stop, wanted him to go on and on, teasing and tantalising her till the inevitable end. But confusion lurked deep inside her, fought for air-space and came out in a rush.

'Louis...no, I don't want you to...to stop...but...' She couldn't finish, couldn't say the one word that she knew would douse his passion like ice-cold water on fire.

She shuddered against him as he pulled her towards him, his hands slithering down to the small of her damp back, drawing her into him.

She wanted to touch the part of him that ground restlessly into her pelvis, wanted to know and familiarise herself with him. To explore and touch and to be free in that exploration. She wanted him to love her as she loved him . . .

'No, Louis,' she implored as his fingers stretched the wet briefs away from her skin.

His lips came back to hers, thrusting and demanding, driving the reluctant spirit from her conscience. She clung to him, the realisation of her tortured thinking rising serpent-like in her mind. She wanted him, could have him at this very moment, but only this moment. Never in her wildest dreams had she anticipated that Love would be such a cruel tormentor. She was falling in love with him, an emotion she hadn't anticipated, didn't want! But how had it happened and so quickly? Life wasn't like that!

'Please, Louis, please stop. I—I can't think . . .'

'I don't want you to think,' he grated harshly. '*I* don't want to think.' His tongue ran over her throat, and smoothed silkily down and down, circling the sweet pleasure-zone of her darkened nipples.

She was losing this battle with her conscience, hated herself for the way she was letting it slip away from her. She fought frantically for a reason that would stand up to the depth of his persuasion, and came up with one, the only one, though it hurt her to have to use it.

She arched herself away from him, the name butterflying on her lips. Her fingers trembled violently as she pressed them into his chest. He anticipated her, steeled his broad chest against her feverish touch. His hands gripped her shoulders and forced her away from him.

'Don't say it, Miranda!' he ground out so fiercely that Catherine's name dropped like a stone from her mouth.

'It has to be said, Louis. You'll hate yourself as much as I already do if you let this go any further.'

'What do you want, Miranda? Forget there is a world out there and tell me what you want at this very moment!' He shook her, furiously, as if it was all her fault.

'What does it matter what I want, what we want?' she blazed, a flash-fire of love and need doused with cold reasoning. 'We don't matter; we are as contemptible as each other. But we aren't the only two people involved. There's Catherine! Catherine! Catherine!' She screamed her name like a purging incantation.

'Damn Catherine!' was the bitter retort that blazed from his mouth.

Shocked and wide-eyed, Miranda stared at him. Louis let out an impassioned groan and gathered her into his arms, holding her tightly against him as if never to let her go.

Miranda clung to him, not understanding and desperate to know. Why was he doing this to her and to himself?

Time and the world stood still as they clung to each other. Seconds, minutes, hours? How long she didn't know or care. There was no passion now, no torrid heat rushing through her, just pain, in her heart and her chest.

Trembling, she forced him away from her, and dared to look up into his eyes.

'We'd better go back,' she whispered, not wanting to but knowing it was the only way.

His shoulders sagged limply. He nodded his dark head. 'I know,' he grated, then his eyes darkened and his hands came up to cradle her face. 'Miranda, don't you want an explanation?'

Oh, she did. But for what reason? What could he possibly say that would ease the ache from her?

'There's nothing you can say that will help,' she murmured. 'I know you think I'm naïve and unworldly but I do understand.' Suddenly she did, bravely she told him. 'We are attracted to each other; even though we've known each other such a short time, there is a chemistry there. A feeling that's as old as time. It happens, has happened, *to us*——'

'And has nothing to do with Catherine,' he interjected.

She shook her head. 'How can you say that? She's there between us like an impenetrable brick wall. You're going to marry her!'

'I'm not.'

Shocked, Miranda stood away from him, her deep brown eyes pained and clouded by that coldly delivered statement.

'I don't understand.'

Had he told her he was engaged to Catherine to warn her off? Was he now tossing aside the intention because of his feelings for her? But what feelings? Bitterness surged through her. He had none, couldn't have, not in such a short space of time. He wanted her, desired her and nothing more...and yet...her feelings went deeper, the dull, agonised thud of her heart told her that.

Louis turned away from her, no explanation, reached down to the hot sand for his T-shirt and trousers. Miranda scrambled into her shorts, her hands shaking uncontrollably in her haste.

The conch-shell. She picked it up, stared at the pink and cream encrustation as if it would offer some answers.

Louis's hands closed over hers and the shell. He seemed to be struggling to put words to his mouth. 'I can't marry her, not now,' he murmured. 'Why do you think I deliberated so long out in the bay at El Paraiso? Why do you think I lied to Catherine about our delay?'

Miranda shook her head again. She didn't want to know, knew the words wouldn't make any difference now. He'd said he didn't want to marry Catherine and she didn't want that on her conscience.

'I wanted you then, desired you more than the woman I was preparing to marry. I wanted you before I'd met you, touched you. I didn't like that feeling and didn't need it. Now it's become too big to fight.'

'So now you don't want Catherine?' Her eyes narrowed, anger spreading like oil on water through her veins. 'And how long before you tire of *me*?' She withdrew her hands from his. 'I'll never give you the opportunity to treat me the way you're treating Catherine; never!'

She had expected a protest, a vague promise that it wouldn't be that way with her, but none came. He just held her eyes for a long second before turning and heading back to the clearing where they'd left the Land Rover.

Miranda followed, subdued into a deep depression. It was all turning out ten times worse than she could ever have imagined. Now she was more of an encumbrance than ever. In the short time here on his island she had affected him deeply enough to ruin his relationship with Catherine. How would Catherine take that? How would they all be able to cope with it?

'Look, this is ridiculous,' she sighed, climbing into the Land Rover next to him. 'What has happened between us shouldn't affect your future with Catherine...'

She saw his knuckles whiten on the steering-wheel. He turned his dark head towards her and fury sparkled his eyes to shards of jet. 'What sort of creature are you? What sort of man do you think I am? This isn't some sort of game. I can't make love to Catherine, don't want to any more. Those are the hard facts. I'm beginning to despise her——'

'Because of me!' Miranda's interruption was spat out with such a force she shocked herself. Regretted it because it indicated she was putting up some sort of fight.

'Yes, because of you!' he admitted harshly.

'No way!' Miranda protested; she wasn't going to be saddled with that. 'You had problems with her before you set eyes on me. If you truly loved her I couldn't have swayed your thinking.'

She bit her lip fiercely. Damn! Why hadn't she seen that coming? Suddenly his intentions were rolling towards her like a de-railed express train. Of course there was a problem in their relationship, one that was nothing to do with her. She was just his excuse, his battering-ram to split the tie between them. He was trying to get rid of Catherine and what easier way to do it than by having another woman in his life? He'd already started, last night, the cut and thrust, using her as his driving wedge in their souring relationship. Ten times worse? Now it was climbing to the hundred mark!

Louis said nothing, started the engine and reversed out of the clearing with a vicious spinning of tyres on gravel.

They didn't speak till they reached the villa and if stage-managed by Louis it couldn't have been orchestrated better. Catherine was pacing the front porch.

'I see you've time to go swanning off with Miranda but no time for me and my coffee-morning,' Catherine screeched.

Louis leapt down from the cab. 'I told you before I had no intention of coming with you. Miranda and I had work to do this morning and then I took her round the island.'

'And had time for a swim, I see.' The blonde woman's eyes locked on Miranda's still damp T-shirt.

'Yes, we had time for a swim,' Louis grated back. 'I showed Miranda the lagoon.'

'What lagoon?'

'The one I offered to show you three weeks ago when you arrived, the one you weren't interested in as swimming doesn't appeal to you.' He reached into the cab of the Land Rover and tossed Miranda the conch-shell.

Taken by surprise, Miranda had no choice but to catch it.

'And I suppose Miranda is the greatest swimmer since Flipper the bloody dolphin!' came the cryptic retort.

Oh, God, stop it, stop it, stop it! Miranda wailed inside.

'She does a fair imitation,' Louis responded coolly, plunging his hands into his pockets and walking towards Catherine.

Miranda saw no more, heard no more, turned and ran round the side of the villa, through the tropical gardens and across the lawns to the beach. She ran till her lungs pleaded for mercy, came to a halt at the outcrop of rocks Louis had kissed her by. She climbed the rocks, tearing at them to get higher and higher and then she stopped, took huge gulps of clean sweet sea air to give her strength. Bracing every muscle in her body, she drew her arm back and flung the conch-shell high in the air.

'You ba-a-astard!' she screamed at the top of her voice as the shell soared and spun and plummeted into the sea.

'In future I'll take my meals in my room,' Miranda told Sunset later in the afternoon.

Sunset was returning a pile of newly altered clothes to Miranda's wardrobe and Miranda was stretched out on the bed, the blinds drawn to keep out the sun.

'Oh,' was all Sunset said. She went through to the dressing-room and hung up the clothes, came back and stood next to the bed. 'Are you sick, Miss Miranda?'

Miranda swung her legs to the floor. 'No, not sick.' What excuse could she give for wanting to eat alone? The truth, that her feelings for Louis were tearing her apart and she couldn't bear to be in the same room as him and the woman he was supposed to be marrying? 'I just thought Louis and Catherine would like some time on their own,' she told Sunset.

The more she thought about it, the more the idea appealed. Maybe with her keeping a low profile they could sort out their differences. She couldn't bear a repeat of last night's performance, not after the matinée this afternoon as well, and now knowing that Louis was hesitant about his love for Catherine it would make the situation all the more stressful.

Miranda's emotions were already drained so Catherine's must be slowly ebbing too. Yes, if she kept out of the way all might be well.

'What shall I say to Mr Louis?'

Miranda looked sharply up at Sunset. Of course, Sunset would have to report back to Louis, make some excuse for her absence at the dinner table to-night; after all, he was lord and master around here.

'Apologise and say I've got a migraine.' Let him think what he liked to that!

'Have you got a migraine?' Sunset queried with laughter in her deep brown eyes.

She couldn't fool Sunset. Miranda grinned up at her. 'No, but you won't tell on me, will you?' It was hardly fair to burden her with a lie but somehow it was unavoidable.

'No, I won't tell.' Sunset didn't probe and Miranda was glad. She didn't want to open up to her; *that* wouldn't be fair.

'I'll ask Naomi to make up a tray for you again. But what about tomorrow; will you still have a migraine?' Sunset giggled.

Miranda couldn't think that far ahead. She'd vowed to herself never to eat with those two again but she couldn't make excuses every night.

'I'll cross that bridge tomorrow,' she told Sunset.

'And tomorrow I'll do your hair,' Sunset said brightly before swinging out of the room.

Miranda was studying the appalling state of her hair in the dressing-table mirror when Louis burst into her room.

'Some migraine! It doesn't prevent you from sitting up and gazing at yourself in the mirror, does it?' He was angry and Miranda couldn't take any more today. She willed a migraine attack, rubbed her forehead to urge it on.

'It's coming,' she told him.

'Funny, but last night you were claiming you don't suffer from them.'

'There's always a first time,' she retorted back.

'And a last time. If you're sick you get no food. Do I make myself clear?' he clipped.

She wished she'd invented a tummy upset now because he obviously didn't believe her, but that wouldn't have got her any food either. 'As clear as ditch-water,' she gibed back dangerously.

'Don't play stupid games with me, Miranda. You'll join us for dinner and that's the end of it. You eat in the dining-room or not at all!'

'I'll starve, then, because there is no way I'm going to risk stomach ulcers with you two at each other's throats all night!' She stood up. 'Now get out of my room and leave me alone!'

'Don't order me around in my own home...'

'It's your home now, is it? Yesterday it was mine too, but apparently my requirements and needs don't count. I refuse, absolutely refuse to be used and humiliated. If you want rid of Catherine, be a man and do it honourably; don't use me in your scheme of things!' She went to escape into the bathroom but he caught her wrist and whirled her round to face him, his features harshly etched with fury.

'Is that what you think? That I'm using you to drive a wedge between me and Catherine?' His tone was so appalled that a twinge of doubt niggled inside Miranda.

'Aren't you? All that garbage about wanting me, not being able to make love to Catherine because of me. All lies. You want Catherine to believe there is something between us so she'll get wildly jealous and . . .'

'Wildly jealous?' Louis dropped her wrist as if she had some contagious disease. 'I'm not believing what I'm hearing! You think I'm using you to make Catherine jealous?'

'Aren't you?' she repeated brusquely.

'I don't have to use you, Miranda—nothing could be further removed from my mind than that. Catherine would resent you if you were Mother Theresa; she resents anything and anyone that occupies my time and keeps me away from her.'

'She must love you very much, then,' Miranda delivered softly, resignedly. If he couldn't see that, he was even more of a snake than she had first thought.

He held her eyes for a long minute, the pulse at his temple throbbing deeply, his skin darkening burgundy under his tan.

He was fighting his conscience and fighting her too. Well, let him battle away; it was his life not hers. She turned to the bathroom and he let her. She heard the gentle swoosh of the patio doors as he slid them shut after him.

Hunger woke Miranda the next morning. Louis had meant what he'd said the night before. If she didn't eat in the dining-room she'd get no food. Her pride wouldn't allow her to join them and she'd stayed in her room feeling like a schoolgirl confined to the dorm on bread and water for cheeking a prefect. Except there hadn't been any bread and water and she'd have been grateful for that.

'So much for the hunger strike,' Louis drawled sarcastically as she sat down at the table by the pool where breakfast was taken every morning.

Almost immediately Naomi appeared with such a huge breakfast of ham, eggs and mushrooms that she expected her to place it in front of Louis. But she set it down in front of Miranda, giving her a grin and a wink. Miranda had to smile.

'I suppose that is some sort of grin of triumph. You might have bewitched the staff but you don't fool me. Don't pull stunts like that again, Miranda. I won't tolerate it.'

'I don't call wanting to eat in my room a stunt. I told you why and I still think the reason was justified. I object to being used, and refuse to allow it to happen again.'

'It won't. Catherine and I have resolved our differences.'

Miranda swallowed hard. How far had they resolved their differences—all the way? The thought, the images of them spending the night together, loving each other, grazed through her like a rusty knife.

'Where is she this morning?' Miranda asked, a devious way of finding out without actually asking if he'd spent the night with her. She was prepared for the answer. Since flinging the conch-shell back to where it came from something had happened inside her, a thin covering of lacquer was hardening up for the next coat. It was the only way she could survive—to brittle her emotions till they were impenetrable. She hadn't even allowed herself space to question whether she was actually in love with him or not. The notion bubbled around in her mind but refused to settle long enough for inquisition.

'Talk of the devil,' Miranda murmured, loud enough for Louis to freeze her with a look that was capable of icing over the equator as Catherine sashayed towards them. She was liberally covered with anti-sun aids as usual, the Florida sunglasses, a wide-brimmed straw hat, metres of floating lawn that covered almost every inch of bare flesh. She was hell-bent on keeping that alabaster look about her.

While Catherine poured herself a cup of hibiscus tea and chatted happily to the two of them, Miranda glanced down at her own long bare legs, the colour and gleam of a ripe chestnut, her bare feet brown and leathery. She slid them out of sight under the table and answered Catherine's question.

'I'd rather not if you don't mind, Catherine, but nice of you to ask me. Perhaps I could meet them another time.'

How hard they were all trying. Catherine programmed to be nice to her and offering to introduce her to her cronies, Louis looking smugly on as if he'd won the Nobel peace prize. And Miranda betraying herself, hating being pleasant to Catherine but nevertheless doing it for want of a quiet life.

'Enjoy your day, you two,' she said pleasantly as she stood up to leave.

'And where do you think you're absconding to?' Louis asked.

'Thought I'd go for a drive and do some shopping.'

'You have money, do you?' sliced Catherine, sucking her cheeks in as if she'd swallowed a lemon whole. So much for her be-nice-to-Miranda resolutions!

'I...no——' Embarrassment powered through Miranda.

'You'll have to put off your shopping trip, Miranda,' Louis interjected to save her. 'We have a lot to get through today.'

Was he still determined to get her occupied with something? Surely yesterday's fiasco had been enough for him? But she didn't argue, didn't want Catherine throwing money in her face again. She hadn't any; one day she'd have to ask Louis for some. She'd go without rather than subject herself to that humiliation, she vowed.

'So what is it today?' Miranda asked when she joined him in the study. 'Keyboard capers for the uninitiated?' She plumped herself down in front of the computer. If she lived to be as old as Methuselah she'd never master this ogre.

'Don't denigrate yourself, Miranda.'

'Why, are you quite capable of doing it for me?' She swivelled in the chair to face him.

'Have I ever put you down?' he said quietly.

'Several times,' she retorted.

'It was never my intention.' His eyes were soft and somehow not fighting her any more. 'Has anyone ever complimented you, praised you for your achievements?'

'What achievements?' Her eyes widened innocently.

'There you go again, bringing yourself down.' He perched on the edge of the desk. 'You're not the useless person you think you are, but you persist in believing it. Why do you do that to yourself?' His voice was soft and persuasive, urging her to open up to him.

Miranda was tempted, too, to spill out all her insecurities; but he wouldn't believe her—why should anyone believe that a girl with her background could feel so useless? But she did and, though she told herself a hundred times that there were people worse off than herself, it didn't help. She had no one, no family, no one close to her to listen and offer advice . . . but Louis was offering. But she was part of an agreement, she reminded herself, and steeled her pride against him.

She leaned forward, propped her elbow on her knee and held her chin in her hand. Her eyes sparkled mischievously.

'Well, yer see, I was loike orphaned.' She put on an outrageous cockney accent. It was the only way to play down his query—to make fun of herself—

then perhaps he would leave it alone. 'An' that makes yer pretty insecure an' then this uncle wiv a load of bread takes me under 'is wing, instead of giving me the luv I wanted 'ee showers me wiv everyfink. Yer get to feel you ain't up to nufink.'

Louis laughed, shook his head in disbelief. 'I don't believe you, Miranda; not for one minute do I believe you.'

Strangely, she'd been laughing with him, desperately trying to lift the depression that was boring down on her; but now her eyes clouded and she grew serious and wanted to talk and unburden herself.

'It's partly true,' she murmured, staring down at the polished pine floor. 'There was never anyone around to tell me I'd done well . . . so what was the point of trying? Uncle Sagan was always too busy and across the other side of the world anyway. He never married so there was never an Aunty Sagan.' She swallowed hard, suffocating those years of feeling so desperately alone. 'Presler . . . Presler's rejecting me coupled with my uncle's being arrested made me see how vulnerable I was—vulnerable . . . and pretty useless without my uncle's money to support me.' Miranda looked up at him. 'I'm not trying to make excuses for myself but it's a fact. I had three months on El Paraiso to ram that home to myself—that and . . .'

'And what?' he urged softly when she didn't go on.

'And you,' she forced out after a lengthy pause. 'I was so proud of myself for coping on that island.

Every day was a challenge, every day a test. Then you burst my bubble by telling me an imbecile could cope...'

'Oh, no, Miranda.' He came across the room, quickly, urgently, squatted in front of her and took her hands in his. 'I would never have said that if I'd known how deeply you felt about it. I didn't know you then, I didn't think it would hurt you. I only wanted to snap you out of your self-pity.' He smiled. 'When I come to think of it I was probably jealous.'

'Jealous?'

'Jealous of how beautifully you did cope on that primitive island. It's every man's dream to escape. Some of the most successful novels in history have been stories of men against the elements, whether a paradise island or climbing a mountain. And you did it—a slip of a girl who'd been brought up in luxury, you survived, and I wonder if I could have done under the same circumstances. I think I would have hitch-hiked back to civilisation after the first night under the stars.'

Miranda smiled. 'Thanks for the compliments but it doesn't help, does it?' She shrugged helplessly. Knowing that secretly he had admired her courage didn't help one bit now, didn't alter the situation. She had to make a future for herself and after yesterday that wasn't going to be easy. 'It's going to take you months to teach me to type,' she added forlornly.

'Teach you to type?' he queried with a frown.

'Well, that's all I'm good for. You were totally unimpressed with my ideas for the coral reefs yesterday and I've got to do something with my time here. Perhaps I can do your letters for you.'

Louis straightened up, a smile creasing his mouth, crossed to his desk and picked up a sheaf of papers. He took them to her, placed them in her lap.

Miranda stared wide-eyed at them, not understanding.

'Faxes from Jamaica, the Bahamas, the Caymans,' he told her. 'When you went to change yesterday I called my contacts, everyone I knew who had an interest in marine preservation. Underwater gardens are being developed everywhere, guided tours of the coral reefs, everything you had suggested. All those people are in the know and sending me details. Those faxes are acknowledgements of my calls and queries.'

'But . . . but you didn't say, you didn't even hint you thought it a good idea!' Miranda was stupefied, her voice creaking with shock.

'Didn't want to raise your hopes before I made my calls; and another reason. You took me by surprise. I hadn't given it a thought and you stunned me with your suggestions.'

Miranda opened and shut her mouth like a fish. She couldn't believe it! He actually liked her idea, was going to put it into action! Her excited eyes darted over the faxes and then she frowned. 'But these are addressed to me?'

Her eyes darted back to him and he gave her a nonchalant shrug of his shoulders. 'It's your baby, not mine.'

'You...you want *me* to run it?'

'Who else? We'll set it up together, a combined effort, and then you can take over if you want to. You're a brilliant swimmer and obviously have a great love of the sea, and if you want to you can go as far as conducting some of those tours yourself.' He shrugged his shoulders again. 'It's up to you how far you involve yourself in the running of it. You can operate the whole set-up from here or go out and be a part of the operations team; the choice is yours.'

'It's unbelievable, totally unbelievable!' she screeched.

'So you'll do it?' he asked, delighted she was so pleased.

Miranda's eyes were so bright with happiness they hurt. Would she do it? It was the greatest thing that had ever happened to her. It would be a success too, she'd make sure of that. It was a challenge, bigger than the survival challenge of El Paraiso. She knew it was going to work, knew it with such a certainty she nearly burst.

She leapt to her feet and impulsively threw herself at Louis, hugged him till he groaned for a reprieve. He'd given a purpose to her life, a goal to go for. Finally she let him go, suddenly embarrassed by her impetuousness. He held her by the shoulders and looked into her eyes.

'I'd hoped you'd be pleased,' he grinned down at her.

'Pleased? I'm over the moon and back. You actually have faith in me—that's the biggest thrill of it all. I'll do it, *we'll* do it, Louis,' she husked. 'I'll work so damned hard I'll run you off your feet.' She was on such a high she felt she was taking off into space.

'Now cool it, Miranda. It sounds like a dream at the moment but it's not going to be easy,' he reasoned sensibly. 'There's going to be a lot of work ahead of us.' He grinned widely. 'I'm afraid you're going to have to learn to type after all.' He nodded towards the computer. 'You're going to have to learn to use that, and the fax, and the copier. It's going to be a hard slog but I've got every confidence in you.'

'But I'll do it, I know I will,' she breathed with such conviction that he believed her.

He was still holding her by the shoulders and she didn't care, didn't object. For a brief spell she forgot Catherine and her own muddled feelings for Louis, why she was here and under whose sufferance.

It all hit her later, washed over her in a brutal wave of despair. She was resting in the heat of the afternoon, resting her body, not her mind—that hadn't stopped spinning with plans and ideas. But now she shot up on the bed as if it were on fire.

It was all an impossible dream. How could they set up this business? How could she run it? She wasn't stupid. It would take time, too much time.

Months to set up, build the chalets, the marinas, organise staff, equipment, advertising... maybe a year, or two or three, several more seasons after that to see it taking off.

Miranda rubbed her burning forehead. What on earth was Louis thinking of in even suggesting the idea? After a year she wouldn't be here. After a year he would have fulfilled his part of the deal with her uncle and she would be free to go!

CHAPTER SEVEN

FOR the first time in her life Miranda was totally
absorbed. Hours sped into days, days into weeks.
She didn't count them; there wasn't time. No time
for personal thought either. It was as if she was
reborn into a world so exciting and fascinating that
there was only room in her mind for Operation
Paradise, as Louis had christened the new project.

She hadn't brought up the time element with
him—how long it was going to take to get it all set
up. She had just let herself be carried along on
Louis's wave of enthusiasm, not wanting to think
any further than the present. And the present was
good, all the work isolating her mind in one
direction only. She needed it and after that initial
spasm of panic wasn't prepared to think what would
happen at the end of her year.

With Louis's outstanding patience she had mas-
tered the ogre—the computer that had appeared so
terrifying at first but now obeyed her every
command and soon let her know when her ten-
tative demands were out of order. She made mis-
takes, huge ones at first, but with two fingers and
occasionally a wayward thumb she coped, to her
surprise and delight.

The fax and the photocopier were building-bricks
in comparison to the intricacies of the computer

game. Miranda loved it all and, better still, Louis was delighted with her progress.

She missed him. Miranda, with a deep sigh, stretched back on a sunbed by the pool one afternoon. She didn't want to miss him but couldn't avoid it. They had worked so closely together that when he had left for her uncle's islands with an architect and surveyor she had felt as if a Siamese twin had been wrenched from her side. In a way she had been hurt, too, had fully expected to accompany him on the trip; but he hadn't made the suggestion and she hadn't asked. So now she was left alone with Catherine and the hours that normally sped like earthbound meteors dragged wearily.

'Haven't you work to do?' Catherine iced as she made herself comfortable on a lounger under a palm-frond umbrella.

Miranda opened one eye. Catherine, like Countess Dracula, usually kept out of the glare of sunlight, which suggested that her company was going to take the form of some sort of blood-letting.

'There isn't much I can do till Louis gets back,' she murmured, closing her quizzical eye against the sun.

'You surprise me. According to Louis you could organise the raising of the *Titanic* while simultaneously piloting the first spacecraft to Mars!'

'Thanks for the compliment,' Miranda uttered back, purposely ignoring the weight of Catherine's sarcasm.

'No compliment, dear. I was implying that without Louis at your beck and call you're pretty useless.'

It had to come. Miranda steeled herself for it. She was surprised it hadn't happened before. Catherine had been suckling this particular grievance till it had finally turned sour on her. With Louis, the mediator, out of the way she was free to let the venom shoot from her fangs. How she had controlled herself for so long Miranda marvelled at; she even admired her for it in a way. Louis had spent every waking, working moment with her and Operation Paradise, and Catherine had seethed—so far kept her opinions to herself, yet nevertheless seethed.

'We need the surveyor's report before we can progress any further,' Miranda told her, not wanting to get drawn into World War Three.

'I really don't see the point of the exercise. Louis has never shown an interest in tourism before. Frankly I think he's taking this agreement with your racketeer uncle too far, but then I suppose he has to act willing. An agreement is an agreement, after all—even with a crook.' Catherine ploughed on, knowing the deep furrows of *angst* she must be swathing through Miranda's heart. 'But then, I expect the whole project will fold like a pack of cards when your term is up. Louis will be joining me in Miami and this little charade will be dead and buried.'

And so the reaper shall harvest. Miranda sowed her own seeds of dissent. 'Not necessarily. I'm enjoying myself so much I might stay on after my year.'

It was the first time the thought had entered her head but if she gave it more time to blossom it might become a possibility. If she could play down her feelings for Louis, maybe find somewhere else to live on the island . . . Depression swamped her. And pigs might fly!

There was a long pause while Catherine germinated her comment. 'You won't be enjoying yourself much longer, dear. Louis is already feeling the strain of his responsibility. He's humouring you. Don't forget he's a businessman. His intentions were to sell those islands on, make himself an enormous profit and goodbye Miranda Gordon. Your ideas have added a nice little bonus, that's all; he'll make a bigger profit now.'

'What . . . what do you mean?' Miranda sat up, not able to lie still a second longer.

Catherine lay motionless on her lounger, save for one limp white hand flaying dismissively in the hot air.

'A viable business concern will rake in more money than four dead islands.'

Where Miranda had got the idea Catherine was a dumb blonde socialite with nothing on her mind but whose dinner party to be seen at next mystified her. She was shrewd, cunningly shrewd. But maybe she wasn't! Miranda's heart beat out a warning. She couldn't have thought that out for herself. She'd been fed it!

No wonder everything had been running smoothly lately. Catherine and Louis were no longer at loggerheads, and the evening meal had become a pleasant and fitting end to those long days of work and more work. She was being used, her ideas being worked on to feather their nests. Catherine was right. Once her year was over Louis could bow her out of his life and sell the islands on, and Operation Paradise along with it to swell the profit. And there was Miranda wondering what on earth would happen to the project at the end of her year!

Miranda got up from the sunbed shakily. How could this woman affect her so? A few well-chosen words uttered so destructively and she was like a jelly. She slipped on her robe and picked up her book and without another word walked away.

It was hours before Louis was due to return and she would have to wait to tackle him. And she would tackle him, demand to know the truth. Though she had a suspicion that Catherine had uttered it already.

'I'm not telling tales!' Miranda blurted furiously.

She should have foreseen this, realised that Louis would take it all the wrong way. She had held back when he had returned. Left Catherine to greet him at the jetty, watched from the veranda as Catherine had launched herself into his arms as if he'd been away for two years instead of two days.

Yes, she had waited—waited for Louis to seek her out in the study where she had taken refuge, not being able to bear to see his arms fold around his fiancée.

'Catherine wouldn't say such a thing, even suggest it. It's totally wrong!' Louis blazed back at her, so angry that his voice ricocheted off the walls like bullets.

'I'm just repeating what she said, not telling tales like a silly kid!' She clenched her fists to stop herself from lashing out at him. She wanted to hurt him as his evasive answers were hurting her. 'Tell me the truth! Did you plan to sell my uncle's islands on?'

'Yes! Originally, I did!'

'And you still want to? You want to sell the islands and Operation Paradise with it...to get...to get more money?'

'Damn you! What do I want with more money?' he shouted furiously, eyes glittering with murderous rage at the suggestion. 'I've enough for three generations after me...'

'So why are you doing this? You know I'm only here for a year. This is going to take longer than that! What are you going to do when I'm gone?'

The anger sagged from him and he rubbed wearily at his brow. Guilt stabbed at her. He was tired after his trip and... Damn him, why should he make her feel guilty?

'I want the truth from you, Louis Mendoza. Are you using me? Do you want to sell those islands or was Catherine, your oh, so wonderful fiancée, trying to cause trouble?'

'How the hell would I know what ticks in a woman's brain?'

'Stop it!' Miranda cried. 'Why won't you give me a straight answer? What are you trying to hide from me?'

There was such a pained, lengthy silence that she wanted to lash out at him again. Why was he treating her this way—teasing and circling her tormented emotions? He had given a new, exciting purpose to her life and now he was snatching it all away from her. The truth was all she asked; was it so very hard to admit to?

Louis moved round the room, settled in his chair behind the desk. 'You want some truths?' he said quietly. 'Well, I'll give them to you. Yes, I had planned on selling the islands on when I made that agreement with your uncle, but I changed my mind...'

'Yes, when you heard my ideas for the reefs! Then it became even more of a glossy prospect——'

'Hear me out, Miranda. Just keep that volatile mouth of yours shut for a minute!'

She clamped her lips together resolutely, and braced herself for what was coming—the truth at last!

'Your ideas had nothing to do with my decision to keep them. I'd already changed my mind before that. Planned the deep-sea fishing from the islands.'

Miranda's stomach churned. That was true. He'd put in a lot of work before she had put up her own ideas; they were just an extension to his.

'Catherine said you'd had no interest in tourism before, so why now—why did you do that?'

Louis's answer was so long in coming that she wondered what lies he was dreaming up to fool her with. 'I want to bring my business interests closer to home...and...'

'And what?' she cried impatiently.

'And I did it for you,' he admitted finally.

She saw it all now, but it didn't change much. 'To give me something to do?' she grazed contemptuously. 'And what a bonus for you! I just happened to come up with a good idea you could poach. So in a year's time when I'm gone you'll sell out anyway. It's just a slight variation on Catherine's idea.'

'It's a world away from Catherine's thoughts. She led you to believe it was money-orientated. After what you've just told me about your conversation with her by the pool I realise she knows the real reason why I want to develop those islands.'

'And what is the real reason? Everyone seems to know what is going on but me!' Miranda exploded.

'I've already told you.' He hesitated again as if battling with himself as to what to tell her. He shrugged hopelessly, losing that inner war. 'I'm doing it because of you. I want to keep those islands to keep you here with me.'

She hadn't heard correctly. The tree-frogs outside thrummed so violently that they blurred his words.

'Me?' It came out in a splutter. 'But why? I don't understand.' She didn't. Since Operation Paradise had been conceived things had gone so well. Her feelings for him had been stifled under a deluge of work and she had thought he'd coped likewise, somehow dealt with his desire for her in a sensible and proper way. He and Catherine had seemed to be happy—not ecstatically so, but they had certainly reached a compromise.

'You should understand, Miranda,' he said sombrely. 'We've both tried to avoid the issue but it's still there. Working so tightly with you has only bonded us together more. Don't deny you feel the same way because I won't believe you.' He rubbed his chin remorsefully. 'But one thing is for sure— the situation can't go on like this.'

'Louis!' Miranda raked her hair from her face, and licked her dry lips. She was still reeling from the shock of his still wanting her, but it didn't alter anything. He was right; it couldn't go on. She was going to do the right thing. 'I'll leave, I'll go, Louis. It's impossible for me to stay.'

'I don't want you to go.' The statement was torn from his soul.

She was angry then. 'What you want doesn't matter! *I* want to go, *Catherine* wants me to go!' Suddenly her eyes filled with tears and she held them back fiercely. 'You're so damned selfish, do you know that? You play with people, worry them like a cat teasing a mouse. I feel sorry for Catherine...'

'Don't waste your pity on Catherine,' he told her gently. 'You were right. We had problems before you stepped into our lives.'

'Yes, it's easy to say that now...'

'It's never easy to admit failure,' he grated harshly. 'This isn't your fault. You and I are a separate issue and it has nothing to do with the relationship between Catherine and myself.' He paused to let her digest that, then went on slowly, 'I've known Catherine for a long time. We met in Miami and it was all different then. A world away from island life. I always had reservations about the transition for her. Now she has admitted she wants to go back to Miami—she prefers the more sophisticated life there. She wants me to go back with her and I can't do that.'

'You would if you loved her enough.'

'Yes, I would if I loved her enough, but I don't. I still care for her enough not to want to hurt her, though.'

'But you are hurting her, Louis,' Miranda argued, the tears still there but not for herself any more.

'It works both ways, Miranda. If her love for me went deeper than my bank balance she'd want to be here with me, but she doesn't. I'm only glad I discovered how cold, calculating and selfish she really is. But if you want to talk about hurt feelings, what about mine? She's hurting me through you. It creases me to hear the abuse she throws at you.'

Miranda shook her head feverishly. 'So you see I am partly to blame. She abuses me because she sees me as a threat. She's unhappy because of me. If I weren't here you might have a chance. I don't want that guilt on my shoulders.'

'It's not your guilt, it's mine. Why do you persist in taking on other people's guilt? You've done it with your uncle's—taken on his crimes as if you'd committed them yourself. You're not to blame for other people's actions. Catherine and I would have split up if you hadn't been here. You have to believe that or there is no hope for us.'

He got up from the desk and came towards her. She didn't want him to touch her and took a step back but there was nowhere to go. He took her shoulders gently.

'Since you came into my life I hardly know myself any more. Those two days out in the bay of El Paraiso were the most difficult of my life. I had Catherine back here waiting for me, you out there wearing your vulnerability like a shroud. I was torn, ravaged by my desire for you and my duty to Catherine, and it was a duty. Catherine came down here to San Paola in an attempt to patch up an already shaky relationship. It's been hopeless. I made a mistake in my life, thought that Catherine was the woman for me, but I was wrong. *I'm* paying for that mistake, not you. I can't marry her...'

'You would have done if it weren't for that crazy agreement with my uncle,' she persisted.

'I wouldn't, Miranda; the doubts were already festering inside me. Had been before you came into my life.'

'You might have stood a chance if I hadn't been around.'

Her repetitive arguments were getting more feeble and she hated the weakness seeping through her. She did believe him, had already realised that there had been problems between them before she had arrived on the scene; but it didn't help. She still felt so terribly bad about it.

'Catherine is leaving tomorrow,' he told her.

If she had been shot at point-blank range the shock couldn't have been more painful and intense.

'No, Louis. You can't let her.'

'It's her choice, and has nothing to do with you. We haven't argued; everything is just fine. She intended going before the rains anyway.'

Miranda stiffened her shoulders and for a second anger flashed in his eyes at her resistance and then he let her go.

'It will be different when she's gone and you know what I mean, don't you?' His gaze was so intent and flecked with determination that she felt apprehension struggling within her.

Suddenly she felt more vulnerable than ever. Catherine was going and there would be just the two of them. Catherine had been their insurmountable barrier; with it removed there would be no holding back.

Miranda turned away from him without answering. She wanted him, loved him, knew it with an intensity that bordered on paranoia, and now it seemed she was about to be free to give her love. But what could he offer her in return, and was she being selfish in wanting more than his passion? Marriage wasn't an issue. She wasn't ready for that sort of commitment but she wanted his love, more than she had wanted anything in her life before.

'I'd better get changed for dinner,' she murmured, and he said nothing as she stepped towards the patio doors and the rose garden. She paused in the still, hot night and turned to look back into the study. He was bent over paperwork as if their conversation had never taken place.

Dinner that night was threatening to turn into another nightmare. It was Catherine's last night and though Naomi had made a superb dinner—roast lamb with cherry sauce and sweet potatoes—nothing could raise Catherine's spirits. It seemed Miranda was the only one to feel for her.

Louis offered little in the way of stimulating conversation and Miranda, verging on mania, tried to keep the conversation flowing. She finally hit the right vein by asking Catherine where she shopped in Miami. From then on the atmosphere wasn't quite so strained.

'No, I won't have another brandy, thank you.' Miranda stood up, resisting the urge to yawn. Catherine was boring her to death with her society name-dropping. Catherine was getting drunk, too, Louis getting more tense by the minute. 'I'm going to bed now. I'll see you in the morning before you leave, Catherine.'

'You bet you will!' came the retort, so sharp that Louis looked up from the brandy he was pouring at the bar.

Miranda and Louis exchanged glances before Miranda murmured her goodnights. She hated leaving him to deal with the irascible, drunken Catherine, but her very presence seemed to be making matters worse.

Miranda didn't go to bed right away. She sat outside her bedroom on the veranda and let the humidity cloak her, soothe her mind. There was no moon; already the storm clouds were gathering to urge Catherine on her way. She wondered what Louis and Catherine were talking about. Had Louis told her their engagement was over, or didn't it need to be said—did they both know it was all hopeless? And did Catherine truly love Louis or was she just a gold-digger as Louis had suggested? The questions and her imagined answers wore her out.

At last Miranda was tired enough for bed. She stood up, stretched lazily and it was then that she heard the raised voices. Louis's and Catherine's.

Miranda stepped into her bedroom, switched on the fan, the low drone obscuring all other sounds. She hated those rows. Whatever Louis might say, she did blame herself for the ghastly eternal triangle they had all found themselves locked in. She had encouraged Louis Mendoza back on the tiny island of El Paraiso, practically thrown herself at him, and that had been the start of all this. She hadn't known then that he already had a mistress back on his island. If she had, she wouldn't have come, never, in spite of the agreement made with her uncle.

It seemed her head had hardly touched the pillow before she was startled awake, her eyes wide and bright with shock and confusion at the crash that filled the room.

'Catherine!' Miranda sat up, pulling the sheet nervously around her. It was daylight but dull, a

gentle hiss of rain outside adding to the horror of
what was going on in her bedroom. Catherine had
gone crazy, flinging her collection of shells around
the room.

'Catherine, stop!'

The furious blonde turned on her. 'It's all your
fault. If it weren't for you, Louis would be coming
back with me.' She stood next to the bed, snatched
at Miranda's sheet and flung it to the floor.

Feverishly Miranda tried to cover her nakedness
with her hands and arms.

'To think he prefers that scrawny body to mine.
Well, not for long, you bitch. I'll get him back...'

'Please, Catherine!' Miranda cried, leaping to a
kneeling position on the bed, the pillow clutched
to her chest to hide her body. 'I've done nothing...'
Surely Louis hadn't told her?

'Nothing? We were going to be married before
you set your grubby feet into our lives.'

'No, don't blame me!' Miranda blazed back, re-
covered now from the initial shock of being woken
so violently. 'You had problems before I arrived.'
How easily it had all changed. Last night she had
blamed herself, this morning she was on the de-
fensive, refusing to take the blame for their
problems.

Catherine raised a fine golden brow. 'Is that what
he told you?' She laughed. 'Men are incredibly un-
original. He told you that to get you in his bed...'

'We haven't...we...' Heat flooded Miranda's
face.

'Next he'll be telling you he loves you and wants
you and needs you and you'll believe him, but it'll
be lies because I know and so do half the women
in Miami...'

'Catherine, don't,' Miranda pleaded. She
couldn't bear all this; it was sickening.

'You didn't know that, did you? That he's left
a string of broken hearts behind him and you'll be
another?' Catherine's eyes narrowed threateningly.
'All the time he's been playing little love games with
you he's still been loving me...' She laughed again
at the look of pain that misted Miranda's eyes. 'Yes,
loving *me*, making love to *me* every night——'

'Catherine!' The roar from the patio doors coin-
cided with a thud of thunder that shook the villa—
or was it one and the same? Miranda squeezed her
eyes tight to shut out the fearful presence of Louis
in the doorway.

'Get out!' Louis roared. 'Get out of this room
before I knock you out!'

Miranda opened her eyes to see Catherine launch
herself at Louis with the viciousness of a lioness
threatened by the hunter. In that instant Miranda
leapt from the bed and ran for the bathroom,
slamming the door and locking it behind her. She
was sick, so violently sick that she nearly collapsed
to the floor as the spasms cramped and tore at her
stomach.

The screaming voice of Catherine receded into
the distance and the pain inside her eased. Miranda
stood for an eternity, grasping the edge of the sink

for support. Catherine's furious accusations swam sickeningly round her head.

Slowly she washed her face, ran her hot wrists under the cold tap to try to allay those terrible fears that haunted her. Was Catherine telling the truth, or was it simply a case of the 'woman scorned' syndrome?

'Miranda, come out. I want to speak to you before I leave.'

Miranda swayed against the sink. Louis. He was going with her after all!

'I have to go before the weather gets too bad. I'll be back this afternoon but I need to speak to you before.'

Miranda flung her robe around her, wrenched open the bathroom door with shaking fingers. A gasp whispered on her lips. Louis stood in front of her, ashen but for a bloody weal down his face and chin.

'I'm taking Catherine and some other people by boat to St Vincent. I want you to forget what happened this morning...'

'How can I forget?' she cried, wanting to throw herself into his arms but not daring to for the confusion that blacked out part of her reasoning. 'I don't know if any of it was the truth or not!' She wondered how much he'd heard—certainly the last part, the truly sickening part. 'What did you tell her about us, Louis?' She shook her head miserably, presuming the worst. 'You shouldn't have; it was cruel, for both of us.'

'I've told her nothing about us, Miranda. But Catherine isn't a fool; maybe I haven't been too smart in hiding the way I look at you, maybe she just senses the chemistry between us. She forgot all the problems in our relationship before you came, but just centred her anger on you. I'm sorry if she hurt you. She was very drunk last night and this morning I suppose all her pent-up feelings erupted. Try and forget it and trust me, Miranda,' he husked. He reached out for her, pulled her violently into his arms and cradled her tousled head against his shoulder.

She clung to him, wanting to trust him, wanting to erase Catherine's wicked accusations from her mind. He nuzzled her hair and then sought her lips with such a desperate, impassioned pressure that they parted willingly. Her hands came up and grasped his hair, her trembling fingers raking through its soft thickness.

She wanted him, there and then, to drive the doubts from her mind, to smooth away the misgivings. Somehow the vicious row with Catherine had heightened her arousal. The erotic pulse that hammered through her wanted gratification, now.

Louis sensed her urgency, teamed it with his own. His mouth ravaged her lips and throat, drawing sweet moans of pleasure from her. She parted her robe for him, threw her head back as his tongue grazed hotly over her nipples, drew on them so fiercely that she nearly drew blood from her own clenched lips. His hands, so determined in their heated exploration, spread over her taut stomach, caressed yet at the same time dug into her flesh with the heat of the passion that powered through him.

He moaned as his hand closed over the soft silky mound that covered her femininity and she cried out with him as he reached the core of her fire and touched its liquid silkiness. Her body shuddered against his and she clutched at the belt of his jeans, twisting her fingers round it desperately and drawing him into her.

'God, Miranda,' his voice husked roughly at her throat. 'I want you now, this minute. I'm crazy about you, want you, need you.'

It was frantic seconds before his words sunk in. He increased the pressure of his fingers, tormenting her with those soft, penetrating thrusts. She couldn't think straight for the raging need that throbbed and pulsed through her, the raging need that was so demanding, verging on the brink of her climax, teetering so deliciously close that to stop would be an agony she wouldn't be able to bear.

But those frantic, heated, pulsing seconds exploded inside her. Not in the mysterious core of her being but deep in her heart, sending shock-waves of white-hot blood coursing through her veins.

His words registered, shocked her brain cells as if a current of electricity had been bolted through them. The words Catherine had predicted she would hear, the words he had spoken to her and 'half the women in Miami...'

'No, Louis!' she cried, lowering her lashes over her eyes so as not to see his face. 'Not now...' She was afraid now. Terrified she had let it go too far and he wouldn't allow it to stop.

'You're right.' His voice was torn from his throat. Miranda opened her eyes, half afraid of what she might read in his. Contempt, dismay, anger. She deserved every one of them. She saw none of them. She saw a look that was totally unreadable.

He lifted his hands to her naked shoulders, bent down and kissed the fading scars of the graze on her shoulder.

'Wait for me, Miranda,' he murmured, kissing her forehead and lifting her robe up around her shoulders to cover her body. His fingers ran softly down one cheek and then he was gone.

Miranda didn't move but to slump back against the wash-basin and let her desire and her strength seep from her body till she was nothing but a limp rag-doll.

He was expecting to return and make love to her, to finalise what had been driving them crazy since the first day they had met. She raised her fevered eyes to the ceiling. She didn't know what to think or do, who to believe or not to believe.

She turned and looked at herself in the mirror. A smear of blood shadowed her chin—Louis's blood drawn by the frenetic Catherine's clawing hands. She rubbed it away viciously, wishing her longing and need for Louis Mendoza were as easily disposable because she sensed she was going to be hurt again.

CHAPTER EIGHT

IT WAS the longest day of Miranda's life, filled with apprehension, confusion and then, as the afternoon dragged on, cold fear.

The weather was worsening, the sea grey and boiling, the heavy cloud pressing the heat down on the island. Miranda's head throbbed with the intensity of the humidity and the fear that Louis wouldn't get back safely.

'Don't vex yourself, Miss Miranda,' Naomi told her. 'Mr Louis knows these waters; he won't take no risks.'

Miranda was glued to the kitchen window, watching the rain lashing it, gazing hopelessly beyond to the jetty, expecting the powerful yacht to come storming back through the heaving seas any minute.

'And no good you watching the jetty,' Sunset laughed, trying to lighten her mood. 'He'll take it into safe harbour at Point Saline and get a taxi back.'

Miranda let her shoulders slump. Of course he would be all right. Silly of her to stress herself so. She turned and got on with the pastry she was rolling for Naomi's pumpkin pie. She'd insisted that she wanted to help, to do something to fill her time. The rain kept them inside and there was nothing she could do in the study till Louis went through the architect's and surveyor's reports with her.

As she worked she wondered what was going through Naomi and Sunset's minds. She'd caught a couple of grins and meaningful looks exchanged between the two but nothing had been said. She supposed her anxious glances out at the jetty had given her feelings away. She sighed. They probably knew everything. Catherine had hardly been discreet while conducting her fearful rows with Louis, had hardly been discreet in showing her dislike and disdain for Miranda.

But both Naomi and Sunset were loyal to Louis and Miranda dared not say anything. Like what? she mused to herself. Louis wanted her, she wanted him, Catherine wanted Louis, and Catherine wanted Miranda dead!

Miranda finished the pastry and excused herself to lie down. Her head was aching badly and she could sympathise with Catherine now. The weather was so oppressive, the rain dismally relentless.

When she awoke it was dark. Naomi had left a covered tray for her in the kitchen. They'd obviously gone home; they both lived in cottages on the estate, and it was obvious they weren't expecting Louis back either. There was no tray for him and Naomi would never leave without making his evening meal.

Depression swamped Miranda as she ate alone in the kitchen. Why hadn't he come back? On an impulse she lifted the kitchen phone. It hadn't been disconnected by the bad weather and she slammed it down furiously. He could have phoned from wherever he was to say he'd been delayed. Or maybe he hadn't been delayed at all...maybe he was snatching time with Catherine...maybe the yacht had gone down in the raging seas...

Dawn broke the next morning with a resounding crash of murderous thunder. Miranda was awake, had hardly slept a wink. Somewhere in the distance she thought she heard a phone ringing but at first put it down to the wind howling and rattling the window-frames. She sat bolt upright. It was a phone ringing. She flew to the hall and grabbed the phone.

'Miranda...?'

The line crackled like frying chips and Miranda shouted down the receiver, 'Louis, Louis!'

'I've been...held up,' came Louis's voice, so far away it sounded as if it was coming from the other side of the world. 'I'm in Miami...'

All the doubts and fears gelled inside her. He was in Miami with Catherine. That hadn't been the plan. Somehow she'd got him back, persuaded him back to Miami!

'Can you hear me, Miranda?'

'Barely.' She banged the phone impatiently but it was useless. His voice was fading away.

'I'll be back tomorrow...' He was gone, his voice having disintegrated with a hiss that had Miranda thumping the phone hysterically. She slammed the receiver down and picked it up immediately. It was as dead as her heart.

All that day she worried the life out of Naomi and Sunset. Did this often happen, the lines put

out by the storm? They both did their best to re-
assure her. Sometimes it was only out for a few
hours. But as the storm and the rain gathered mo-
mentum they finally had to admit that it might be
days.

If she had thought the last day had dragged, this
one was worse. Now she had more painful fears to
torment herself with. Catherine and Louis together
in Miami, Catherine fighting to win back Louis's
love. Catherine winning.

He came back early the next morning. Miranda
was in bed, hot and restless after a feverish night,
listening to the swish of tyres on the front drive.
She didn't get up and run to the front porch as
she'd imagined a hundred times she would. She
stayed where she was, her heart pumping
irregularly.

She heard the huge oak front door shut, suspiciously softly. She strained her ears but heard
nothing more.

Later she crept out into the hallway, crossed to
his bedroom and gently opened the door. He was
asleep on the bed. Sprawled face down, his arms
arced above his head, a sheet covering him from
the waist down. She shut the door, tears pricking
at her eyelids. He hadn't given her a thought. Had
stolen into his room with a guilty conscience, and
he had one, that was for sure. Miranda curbed the
tears. No way was she going to shed a tear over
him! Damn him to hell!

* * *

'There you are.' Louis stepped into the study from the patio. There was a respite from the teeming rain, the sun battling between resolute storm clouds. But there was no respite in Miranda's heart. She'd sat numbly in the study waiting for him to rouse himself, her mind agonising her predicament till she couldn't think straight. And now here he was with an audacious smile on his face.

'And where else would I be but in my prison?' she flung at him stonily.

He frowned, confusion creasing his brow, twisting his mouth.

If he was expecting a warm welcome he had miserably underestimated her; her eyes blazed daggers at him.

'Miranda...' he murmured.

'Don't Miranda me! What the hell were you doing in Miami? Or is that a really dumb question? One I shouldn't expect an honest answer to?'

'I had some unfinished business to attend to——' he began, his mouth narrowing.

'And no prizes for guessing who with! So you chose to spend one last night with your ex-mistress...'

The change in his expression halted her accusations. A pulse of fear penetrated her vicious thoughts.

'Like hell I did!' he raged, coming towards her as if to strike her. 'What the hell's got into you?'

'Don't touch me!' she cried, leaping up from the chair and hurtling across the room, putting the desk between him and his sudden fury. 'You crept in here

in the early hours of the morning, and if that wasn't
nursing a guilty conscience I don't know what was!'

'Good God! What's got into you, Miranda? I
crept in because I didn't want to disturb you——'

'I don't believe you! You couldn't face me...'
Her eyes scathed his with contempt. 'You were
having a last fling with Catherine. Or wasn't it the
last fling? Do you intend to go on seeing her,
whenever business calls you to Miami? Or have you
suddenly decided you prefer her to me?'

In a sudden, furious movement that caught her
unawares he reached across the desk, grabbed her
arm and hauled her round the edge of the desk to
face him.

'I don't need all this!' he seethed angrily, his
hands tightening around her upper arms, hunching
her shoulders painfully. 'I've just got rid of one
praying mantis and I'm landed with another. Who
the hell do you think you are to make such filthy
accusations?'

'Deny it, then!' she ground out between white
lips, her eyes as black with fury as his.

'I shouldn't have to deny it!' he blazed.

'Huh, that's an easy get-out, isn't it? Try and
twist everything round to make me feel the accuser,
the wronged one. You're good at that. You
probably did the very same thing to Catherine—
made it look as if she was in the wrong not wanting
to share your island life with you...'

'Shut up, Miranda! I wasn't with Catherine last
night or any other night since you came here. Can't

you believe that? Your accusations are crazy; you don't know what you are saying!'

'I know exactly what I'm saying!' Suddenly all those pent-up feelings and emotions she'd harboured, waiting for him to come back, bubbled out of control like a white-hot volcano. Tears flew to her eyes. 'Poor bloody Catherine, poor Miranda!' she cried, thumping her chest. 'I understand her now. No wonder she acted the way she did. You rouse in me the same viciousness, the same uncertainties.'

Blind fury and pain drove her across the room. She tore through the open doors of the study. She had to get away, as far from him as possible!

'Miranda!' Louis shouted after her, but she sped on, down to the beach, regardless of the now driving rain, the howl of the wind that spun her hair furiously around her face.

He caught her by the rocks, the place she had run to before. He'd caught her then...had nearly——

'Don't come near me!' she cried with a sob. Out of the corner of her terrified eyes she saw something in the sand. The conch-shell, the one she had flung out to sea and now the turbulent waters had flung it back to her. The tender moment when Louis had presented it to her misted her eyes for a brief second and then she lunged for it, grasped it in one hand and held it up.

'You touch me and I'll swear I'll use this!'

'Drop it, Miranda, or so help me I won't be responsible for my actions!'

His whole body steeled with fury in front of her eyes. He was so overwhelmingly powerful that she hesitated, but only briefly. There was a time-bomb inside her, ready to explode, and she couldn't control it. Love, hate, both fused dangerously till a red mist flashed in front of her eyes. She was no longer in control...

'I warned you!'

His words were like the crack of the gun she had used on him at El Paraiso, the impact of the re-bounding barrel felt in her stomach not her shoulder as he wrestled her to the sand. He pinned her hands above her, sat astride her as she thrashed from side to side beneath him. The sand was horribly wet beneath her with him so—so hot above her.

'Oh, no...' A moan of despair was torn from her throat as the time-bomb of desire unwillingly exploded inside her. 'You can't!' she screamed helplessly.

'Take can't for will, Miranda,' he husked roughly, 'because enough is enough. This fighting is coming to an end in the only way possible. I don't know what's got into you but I know the cure for it.' His mouth swooped to hers.

Miranda tore her mouth from his. 'You...you bastard!'

'You won't be screaming that for long, sweetheart!'

One hand held her wrists so fiercely that to struggle would splinter her bones, the other lifted her T-shirt and exposed her naked breasts to the driving rain, the effect so terrifyingly sensual that she arched involuntarily under him.

It was all Louis needed to soften his approach, gauging it down to soft, stimulating caresses of her taut nipples. When he lowered his mouth to hers once again his anger was gone, superseded by something infinitely more dangerous. Raw intent powered him now as his mouth worked over hers, driving her resistance to despair.

Miranda didn't want it this way and yet there was a part of her that screamed out for this violent assault on her senses, on her flesh. Every nerve-end was on fire, blazing new ground she had never experienced before in her life. Possession flashed through her mind, appalling her and thrilling her at the same time. She struggled once more, as he drew back from her to look into her eyes, as his hand moved to her damp skirt.

Her head tossed from side to side, feverishly, as if trying to shake off a deathly nightmare; yet this was no nightmare, his hand stroking her wet thighs.

He sat back on his haunches, letting go of her wrists, knowing she wouldn't struggle any more. She opened her eyes to see his face, streaming with water, plastering his thick hair across his forehead. His eyes were glittering darkly, aroused to suffering-point. Miranda couldn't move, shocked by her own arousal and his. Oh, God, he was magnificent, straddling her, a predatory animal ready for the kill. Feverishly she brought her arms up and grazed them over his shoulders, her fingernails biting into hard muscle. His rain-soaked shirt clung

to his chest and she ran her hands down the front,
fumbling with the buttons.

'Am I still a bastard?' he breathed hotly down
at her, ripping the shirt from her fingers as she
struggled hopelessly. Then his hands went to the
top of his jeans...

'Bigger than ever,' she murmured.

With a glint of triumph in his mocking eyes he
came down to her, took her mouth so roughly that
she parted her lips, her teeth sinking into the soft
flesh of his mouth, drawing hard on him, willing
him on. Her hands clawed at his clothes, he at hers,
raising her hips to ease her briefs from her heated
flesh.

A sob tore from her lips as he shifted across her
and caressed her inner thighs, higher and higher till
the fire blazed out of control. Fiercely she drew
him down to her, grasping his hips, crying his name.

Suddenly he was inside her with a cry of triumph,
so quickly, so shockingly abrupt that her fingers
clawed at his back. And then he lifted his body up
and with his hands planted firmly each side of her
moved slowly, teasing her, tantalising her till she
was sobbing with heated desire. Daringly she
opened her eyes and watched his face as he moved
in and out of her, fascinated by the contortions of
passion that flexed the muscles of his glistening
body and face, fascinated by the new passions that
rose and rose inside her.

The rain washed over them, dripping from his
face to her breasts. A mist of sensual perspiration
mingled with the raindrops on her upper lip as his

pace increased, driving against her as the rain drove against his own back.

And then she knew, in a huge, glorious bubble of fever deep inside, she knew the mysterious secret that had evaded her before. The ultimate sensation, the power and the sweet agony of consummated love, complete and whole and bursting into showers of flame through her.

'Louis!' she screamed, grasping him into her, pulling him down to her.

'I know, darling,' he gritted, the words torn from his throat. 'I . . . know.'

And then he was with her, suspended by time and passion in a liquid void of heat and thrust that spiralled them out of control in a spinning paroxysm of blazing victory.

Miranda cried then, huge sobs that drained her last breath of strength. Louis lay beside her in the wet sand, his ragged breath gauging down to deep, soft moans of comfort.

'I'm sorry...my darling Miranda...I'm so sorry.'

She clung to him, breathing kisses over his wet face. 'Sorry for the inevitable?' She held his face between her hands and smiled through her tears. 'I'm not crying because I'm sad,' she told him. 'I'm . . . I'm ashamed of myself...'

'Ashamed of your passion?' His mouth grazed over hers, his lips smoothing the rain from her mouth, her face, her eyes. 'Never be ashamed of that.'

'No, not that. I was so afraid of losing you...when you didn't come back... I thought Catherine had won...'

'It wasn't a contest between you, Miranda.'

'I know, I know.' She bit her lip. 'But I was so afraid...I thought you were with her...convinced myself I'd lost you. I was so confused.'

He held her hard against him, smoothing the warm rain from her hair. 'You poor darling, so full of insecurity you can't trust any more. When will you realise it's you I want, no one else but you?'

She broke out into fresh sobs. How could she have mistrusted him so?

'Hush now,' he murmured throatily. 'It's all behind us now, Miranda. Let's start our life together, now, forget everyone and everything but ourselves.'

His lips on hers led the way to a new beginning. She trembled with joy at the prospect of life and love with him.

He laughed softly against her. 'Are we crazy or not?'

She blinked open her eyes as he shifted away from her and stood up. Water coursed down his beautiful naked body, trickling channels through the sand clinging to him.

'I think we must be out of our minds,' she giggled, scrambling to her feet and shivering with discomfort. Sand ground into her flesh, water poured from her face and suddenly she was cold.

Louis struggled into his sopping clothes and then reached down into the sand. 'Here, another conch for your collection.' He tossed it to her with a grin.

Miranda caught it and turned it over in her hands. She didn't tell him it was the same one. Like a boomerang it had happened back into her life. She clutched it to her chest. She'd never let it go again, just as she would never let Louis go. He was her life from now on.

Hand in hand they trudged back to the villa through the driving rain, lost in their own thoughts till a shout from the veranda broke into them.

'Telephone, Mr Louis!' Naomi cried, waving her hand urgently.

Louis kissed Miranda's forehead. 'Get a shower, darling, while I take this.' He left her and broke into a trot along the veranda.

Miranda stripped off her sand-encrusted skirt and top and stood under the hot shower, let the fierce jet soothe her battered, love-sated body. She shampooed her hair, shorter now as Sunset had trimmed away the split ends, glossier too with the rich coconut oil she had massaged in. The new Miranda, contented and more fulfilled than ever before in her life.

This was happiness, pure and simple. Louis wanted her, she wanted him and that was all that mattered in the world. She hummed to herself as she dried her hair in front of the dressing-table mirror.

'Sunset?' Miranda caught her reflection in the mirror and spun on the chair to face her. Sunset's hands twisted nervously in front of her. She took a hesitant step forward and Miranda's heart stilled. Something was wrong.

'What is it?' she whispered.

'Mr Louis said I was to pack your things...'

'Pack?' Miranda husked, not believing it. Her fingers wrapped round the blow-drier she'd snapped off when she'd caught sight of Sunset. God! He wanted her to go. But why? Her heartbeat picked up. Was he regretting their lovemaking already? He'd apologised enough after... He was disappointed... had expected her to be a better lover... Shock and bitterness fought for space in her turmoiled mind.

'Where is he?' she asked of Sunset, her lips drawn into a tight line of fear. This wasn't happening; it couldn't!

'In the study, on the telephone arranging a flight. He said to get ready and he would come and explain. Miss Miranda...'

Miranda didn't wait to hear any more; she rushed from the room, belting her robe tightly around her waist as she ran. A flight? To where? What was happening?

She burst into the study, stopped dead in the doorway. Her tortured thoughts hadn't prepared her for this. Louis sitting at the desk with his head in his hands.

'Louis,' she whispered, stepping towards him, the fight gone from her, painful apprehension superseding it.

He looked up, eyes expressionless, facial muscles taut and unrelenting. Then he got up and came to her, took her hands in his. 'We have to leave immediately, Miranda.'

'I don't understand,' she whispered, confusion and fear knotting hysterically in her stomach.

'Your uncle has had a heart attack...'

The room spun sickeningly around her.

The last leg of the journey was the worst. So near and yet so far. Miranda could think clearly now. The cab sped them through the darkened streets of the city to the private Miami clinic the prison had transferred Sagan Gordon to.

Miranda traced her nervous fingers down the seam of her silk suit and stared bleakly ahead.

'It must be serious,' she murmured to Louis. 'They wouldn't have transferred him to a hospital outside the prison if it weren't.'

Louis shrugged beside her, as exhausted as her by the long, complicated journey from San Paola to Florida.

'I don't know how the system works but I think we must prepare ourselves for the worst,' he told her sensibly.

Time for reassurances was over. Louis had tried to play down the seriousness of the attack but had given up when he'd realised how well Miranda was standing up to the shock of that telephone call from the hospital. They both knew the strain the trial had put on Sagan. He wasn't a young man and

after living a high-powered life of luxury all his life
prison would have had a devastating effect on him.

'I wish I hadn't left Miami...'

'Don't, Miranda,' Louis grated, trying to keep
the edge out of his voice.

Miranda squeezed his hand tightly. They'd been
through all this on the frenetic trip here. Her guilt
and remorse, the if-onlys that had sprung to her
lips every time she opened her mouth. She had exhausted him, herself too. Now all she could feel
was a numbness spreading inside her.

As soon as they arrived they were shown to the
cool intensive care unit. Miranda steeled herself
before going in. Louis stood back and Miranda
understood. She was on her own again. Had it ever
been any different?

She held back her shock as she saw her uncle
propped up in bed, so old and sick, surrounded by
hospital paraphernalia. Monitors were wired to the
now slight body, bleeping threateningly. She knew
he was dying, smelled it as she took his papery hand
in hers and leaned over him to kiss his grey temples.

He opened his watery eyes and smiled up at her.
'I hoped you would get here in time,' he croaked.

Bravely Miranda smiled. 'You're going to be all
right, Uncle.'

'Sure I am.' He squeezed her hand as best he
could. 'You're looking good, Miranda. Island life
suits you...' He struggled for breath and Miranda
bit her lip to force back the tears.

'Don't say anything, Uncle Sagan.'

'What the hell,' he croaked. 'Things have to be said. Not long now. I got your letters. Glad it's all working out for you. Can you forgive me for handing you over to that rogue Mendoza?'

'I understand why you did it,' Miranda smiled through her tears. 'You've always looked after my welfare.'

He sighed. 'Not always in the right way, though. I should have given you more time when you were growing up. Truth is, I never understood kids, never having had any of my own.'

'You did OK,' Miranda said softly. 'You gave me the best a girl could have.'

'Yes, but did I do right for you with Mendoza?' His brow creased and Miranda wondered if he was in pain. 'Never had a damned conscience in my life, but being locked up for hours gives you a time to think. Your letters helped. You seemed happy enough, so the marriage could work...'

'M-Marriage?' Miranda didn't understand. Her skin felt as if it were on fire.

He drew his hand from hers to pat it gently. 'The islands were all I had left to buy your future...'

'Oh, Uncle, you didn't have to do anything. I would have been all right.'

He smiled weakly. 'I didn't want to leave you penniless but I had no choice. I lost everything but those islands. The marriage deal with Mendoza was the best I could do...' He paused to lick his lips and Miranda's mind spun crazily. Penniless? He had put the money in trust for her—her pot of gold at the end of the rainbow, Louis had said. And a marriage deal? Louis had denied that. So what did her uncle mean?

'I didn't want to leave you alone in the world...' Sagan went on, struggling for every word. 'I like Mendoza even though he drives a hard bargain. It took him a long time to come around to my way of thinking but at last I got my own way. I trust him to do the best by you. You understand, don't you?' His voice faded away and Miranda slid off the edge of the bed in alarm.

A gentle hand at her elbow reassured her. She swung her head to face a doctor. 'He's very weak and needs rest,' he told her. 'We have a room prepared for you next door. I'll let you know when he wakes.'

Numbly Miranda allowed herself to be led away from the bedside. Louis leapt to his feet from a chair outside the room and came towards her.

'How is he?' he asked the doctor, folding an arm round Miranda's shoulders.

'I'll be honest: he isn't expected to make it through the night. There's a room next door you can use. I'll arrange for food to be sent and of course we'll keep you informed of his progress.' His bleeper sounded and he excused himself.

As soon as he'd gone Miranda moved out of the circle of Louis's arm. 'There's no need for you to stay,' she murmured. 'I'd rather be on my own.' She looked at him then, so confused by her uncle's words that she didn't know what she was looking for in Louis's eyes. She wanted an answer, a loving reassurance, maybe, that her uncle hadn't known what he was saying; but now wasn't the time and the place to probe.

'I wouldn't dream of leaving you,' Louis told her gently.

Miranda raked the hair from her blazing forehead, braved a smile. 'I'll be all right.' She glanced out into the dark night. 'It's late. It's been a long day and your second trip back here; you must be exhausted.' She wondered why she should be so concerned for his welfare but, in spite of what she now knew, she was. 'I'll call you at the hotel if anything happens.'

He didn't argue, just nodded his dark head and smiled wearily. 'I'll be back first thing in the morning. Are you sure you'll be all right?'

She nodded and said no more. She watched him walk down the corridor, her heart torn, her nerves strained trying to stop herself running after him, begging for answers. Had there been a marriage deal between him and her uncle? Had Louis lied to her about the end of the rainbow? Was she that pot of gold, Louis Mendoza's prize in exchange for the islands?

Slowly she opened the door of the room next to her uncle's. Walked across the thick carpet and gazed hopelessly out of the window. Stars, moon, black sky. Was there an answer out there somewhere? She felt betrayed. Selfishly she willed her uncle to recover to give her the answers to the questions she didn't dare put to the man she loved. Had she been traded for those damned islands?

She was woken in the small hours of the morning by the same doctor. She struggled to her feet from the bed where she had been lying, snatching at sleep to try to blot out the thoughts that tormented her so cruelly. She was still dressed, her clothes crumpled.

The doctor said nothing but she knew by his eyes that the time was near. She was afraid then, terribly afraid, and wanted Louis with her, to hold her, to love her. She swallowed back her fear; Louis would be of no help to her now, or ever. She followed the doctor to her uncle's bedside.

Ten minutes later Sagan Gordon slipped away, peacefully, without pain. Ten minutes in which Miranda had caressed his hand and relived every minute she had ever spent with him. She made her peace with him in that time, forgave him in her heart for his last desperate effort to do right by her. He would never know the pain he had left her with, couldn't have envisaged that she would have fallen so helplessly in love with the man who in cold, hard facts had agreed to marry her in exchange for a necklace of islands. Her uncle had thought he was doing his best for her because in his world he knew no different. Business was business whether it was commodities or souls.

Miranda kissed her uncle's brow for the last time and when she walked from his bedside she knew she was a changed person. She couldn't even cry; that was the measure of her new reserve. No more tears for anyone in her life again . . . and that went doubly for the man who had betrayed her heart— Louis Mendoza.

CHAPTER NINE

MIRANDA left the hospital in a daze. Picked up a cab outside in the street and went straight to the hotel Louis had arranged from San Paola. She checked in and went up to the suite. It was still early, but the sun was shining brightly. She let herself in and closed the door quietly behind her so as not to disturb Louis. She wasn't ready for him yet. She needed more time.

She showered, but felt no better for it, huddled into her dressing-gown and curled herself in a chair by the tenth-floor window. She stared bleakly out at Miami sprawled expensively below her, the creamy beach and blue bay beyond.

She flinched when Louis spoke her name, her nerves raw with pain. She turned and looked up at him standing next to her in his towelling robe.

'He died early this morning,' she murmured and looked away from him.

He smoothed his hand over her shoulder and when he spoke his voice was thick. 'I'm sorry, darling.'

Darling? How could he call her that? After what her uncle had told her it sounded more like a curse than an endearment. She hated him but, still in shock over her uncle's death, she hadn't the strength or the will to tell him.

'I have arrangements to make,' she said curtly, and went to get up. The pressure increased on her shoulder.

'Stay where you are. I'll see to everything,' he told her quietly.

She let him because there was no fight left in her. The numbness deep inside swelled and spread to her mind, closed it off from reality.

She didn't know how long she sat by the window. Louis moved around the suite, making phone calls, trying to encourage her to eat and drink. She refused, shook her head dismally and pleaded to be left alone. Eventually he persuaded her into bed and covered her with a sheet before kissing her forehead lightly.

Miranda was still numb days later. The funeral was over, an ordeal she had got through with Louis at her side. She didn't know what she would have done without him. He'd organised everything. He'd tried to draw her out of her shell, too, but Miranda had hidden herself deep inside her grief and refused to be drawn. She didn't want to talk yet, dreaded the confrontation with him that would end in the inevitable—heated accusations and harsh words that would finally end their relationship.

He didn't love her; had he ever said he had? He had seduced her in more ways than one, because it made it easier for him. He had seduced her into falling in love with him and that was somehow worse than seducing her body. He was ruthless and clever. If she was in love with him half his battle was over—an adoring wife would make life simpler. She didn't doubt that he would ask her to marry him. Wasn't that the agreement—the islands for marriage to Sagan Gordon's niece?

'Miranda, let go, will you? You're bottling it all up inside you. You haven't cried since your uncle died and it's not good for you.'

Her eyes flickered uncertainly as he poured coffee. More coffee. She was awash with it. Suddenly the suite was oppressively claustrophobic. She wanted out—of this suite and his life.

She got up and moved to the window. He came and stood behind her, slid his arms around her waist. She stiffened instinctively. He had barely touched her since they had arrived. They'd slept apart, Louis showing respect for her grief and she had admired him for that at least. She moved away from him and went back to her chair and her coffee.

'Miranda, don't block me out this way,' he said gently. 'I understand how you feel. Grief affects people in different ways but it's over now. Your uncle is at rest and we have to think of ourselves now. I want us to go back to San Paola as soon as possible.'

She slammed her coffee-cup into the saucer and turned blazing eyes up to him towering over her. 'You have to be joking! I'm going nowhere with you, not now, not ever! It's over, Louis. My uncle is dead so now we can forget that wretched agreement.'

Louis frowned at her anger, not understanding. 'The agreement doesn't come into this, Miranda...'

She laughed, without humour. 'The agreement is *this*! It's all it's ever been. If my uncle hadn't died you would have executed it down to the last small print. Well, now you're off the hook: the islands are yours, you can have them but not me. I'll never marry you.'

His eyes darkened warily. 'I've not asked you...'

'It would only have been a matter of time,' she bit out. 'No doubt you would have done it by now if he hadn't had that heart attack. I wonder how long it would have taken you? Two minutes after you took me down on that beach...'

He swung her up from the seat, held her arms as his dark eyes lashed hers with jet fury. 'Took you? You were more than willing, and what's all this marriage business——?'

'That's exactly what it is, what it's always been...business!' she interrupted ferociously. 'And don't put on that shocked, hurt expression. You know exactly what I'm talking about.'

He let her go, sharply, and stood in front of her, every facial muscle taut as strung wire. 'I see it all now,' he grated harshly. 'Death-bed confession, was it?'

'Don't be so bloody irreverent!' It was all she could throw at him, for suddenly she knew he wasn't going to deny it. Somehow she had hoped he would, explain to her that it was all some horrible misunderstanding and that he loved her and everything was going to be all right.

'So all this moping around was for my benefit, not grief for the loss of your uncle? You want to punish me for something your uncle inflicted on the pair of us?'

Miranda went limp. 'You're not denying it?' she husked weakly. So it was all true and the truth was hurting.

'No, I'm not going to deny it. I don't know what your uncle told you but it's obvious that since you mention marriage you know the truth. But what you don't know is that I had no intention of marrying you—not at first, that is!'

She stepped back from him, shocked, hurt stabbing through her. 'I don't understand.'

'You never do!' His anger didn't let up. 'That's the trouble with you, Miranda. You don't try to understand and you never see what is right in front of your face. You have no trust. I had no intention of marrying you under the terms of such an agreement and I told your uncle that on numerous occasions...'

'So you're saying that he lied?'

Suddenly he wasn't angry any more—tense but not angry. His hand jerked up to rake through his hair. 'No, he didn't lie.' His black eyes levelled with hers, willing her to understand. 'When I met your uncle a year before his arrest he put that proposal to me when I said I wanted to buy the islands. He wanted to secure your future. I refused but put the suggestion to him that, if he was so concerned for your welfare, he put the money I was willing to pay for the islands in a trust fund for you, to be paid to you if and when he was convicted. It wasn't enough for him. He didn't want you to be out on your own, with or without money. He suggested that a year's trial might change my mind. He told me how beautiful you were, what a social asset you could be to me, but still I refused. You could have been a goddess for all I cared, but no one forces me into marriage that way.'

'But you did agree in the end,' Miranda murmured.

'I agreed in the end, yes. But before you jump to any more conclusions listen to my side of the story. I liked your uncle, though I despised some of his business dealings. I understood what he was trying to achieve for you. Without him you were alone in the world and he cared enough for you to secure your future the only way he knew how. But I wasn't prepared to commit myself to marriage to someone I didn't know, didn't love. As in all business dealings we wrangled and came up with a compromise. He knew his time was short, knew that one day soon he would be arrested, so he agreed my terms with a few provisos from himself.'

'And—and what were those provisos?' Miranda asked weakly.

'That I would take you for that year——'

'On trial! To see if you liked me enough to agree to the rest of his conditions: marriage!' she blurted.

'Not exactly,' he said quietly.

'Well, it is or it isn't! You can't sit on the fence with this one, Louis Mendoza. Did you agree to marry me for the islands or not?' she almost screamed.

'It wasn't as simple as that . . .'

'You bastard!' she breathed hotly. When he had started his explanation she had nursed hope—now there was none. He was evading the truth and that was all-condemning.

'I agreed provisionally,' he went on patiently, undaunted by her abuse. 'I paid for those islands and they were mine, nothing could change that, but your uncle tied me up with the contract so that I would never have been able to sell them on as I planned; neither could I develop them unless I agreed to marry you. I wasn't prepared for that but I went ahead nevertheless, hoping that one day he might release me from those clauses, that one day I could prove to him that you could stand on your own two feet and make him see the idiocy of expecting me to marry you to protect you.'

'But you didn't have time to prove that, did you? You couldn't wait to develop those islands, especially when I came up with such a great idea for the coral reefs. So you agreed his terms, agreed to marry me?' Miranda croaked helplessly. 'We've been working on Operation Paradise for weeks now. You went to the islands with the architect, the surveyor—you went through all that because you *knew* you were going to marry me.'

'Not exactly——'

'Not exactly? It isn't as simple as that!' she angrily echoed his evasions. 'Why won't you give me a straight answer?'

'Because I know you well enough to know that you won't believe me. Why should you? You are still wrapped up in your own hurt and mistrust.

Until you let go of all your hang-ups there'll be no getting through to you.'

'Try me!' she exploded.

He was hating every minute of this, Miranda knew, hating it because he couldn't talk his way out of it.

'I went through the motions of Operation Paradise for you. You were partly right in that assumption. It was to give you something to do, something worthwhile to occupy yourself with. But by then I was hopelessly in love with you and knew that I could go through with your uncle's demands and marry you and get full control of the islands — but not because I needed them, as you suppose, but because I wanted them for you, for us. I've told you before, I want to loosen up on my commitments in Miami, want to be closer to home...never more than since meeting you.'

Miranda slumped back down into the chair, buried her face in her hands. So it was out, half the truth. He wanted her simply to get final control of the islands. The bit about loving her was a lie, a wicked lie to win her over and make her see his selfish point of view.

'That's what I was doing here in Miami a few days ago. Winding up my financial dealings here, telling your uncle that I was prepared to marry you.'

She raised pained eyes to his. 'And to get him to honour his agreement and hand the islands over to you, unrestricted, so you could do what Catherine suggested—sell them for some colossal amount.'

'Never, Miranda. That was never my intention,' he grated, his brow drawn darkly, his face gaunt with fatigue. 'Why won't you believe me? I want to develop those islands for us and our future life together.'

She responded to that with a cynical smile. 'You've won, Louis Mendoza. You've got the damned islands and you can do what you please with them, and now because my uncle is dead you don't have to honour that agreement and marry me after all.'

'But I want to,' he admitted simply.

Her bitter laugh came out in a croak. 'What a warped sense of honour you have. You have what you want; you don't need me any more.'

'I need you more than ever,' he told her gravely. 'Without you I don't want any part of the whole operation. I love you and want you and need you.'

She looked up at him, eyes glazed with fever. She'd heard those words before and, as Catherine had so rightly said, so had half the women in Miami. She shrugged her shoulders dismissively, a gesture to hurt him. 'Very touching, I'm sure, but there is one thing your devious, calculating mind has overlooked. I don't love *you*, want *you* or need *you*—so get lost!'

Colour rose brutally under his dark skin and for a brief moment she thought she had hurt him; but of course she had, her hardened mind reasoned. She'd hurt the pride that beat in place of his heart. Rejection never came easy to cruel, grasping men like him.

He held her defiant brown eyes for an agonised minute and when he finally spoke his tone was iced with bitterness. 'I misjudged you, thought something warm and caring pulsed deep inside you, but now I realise you are as lacking in feeling as a brown paper bag. You have your life back, Miranda; I give it to you without my blessing—you don't need it. You're quite capable of tackling the world on your own bitter terms.' He reached into the inside pocket of his jacket and took out a card, tossed it down into her lap. 'My lawyer's phone number. Get in touch with him and he'll hand over the money I put in trust for you.'

'Where are you going?' she cried as he reached the door, leaping to her feet. He couldn't just walk out like this, he couldn't!

He turned to her, gave her one last hostile look of derision and told her, 'To get on with my life, sweetheart! I've wasted enough time on you and your supposedly crushed emotions.' He closed the door softly behind him.

She had expected to cry at least, but nothing came. Not that day or the next or the one after that. Not one heated salty drop to wash away her love. At first she had been consumed with rage and indignation, then the numbness had seeped back, leaving her weak with struggling against her love. She still loved him, always would, and that was another confusion to sap her strength. How could she still want him after what he had done?

She wouldn't touch his money, of course, though she reasoned that she was entitled to it because it was her uncle's, after all. But it was tainted money and how could she spend it knowing it had been thrown at her as if she were one of Catherine's charity cases?

Would he go back to her? she wondered, but dismissed the thought on the grounds of the severe pain it knifed through her to think about it.

She took the lift down to the hotel coffee-shop, a habit she had forced on herself every afternoon in a feverish attempt to drum some life into herself. Not that there was much life in the coffee-shop, but it was a beginning, she told herself as she sat down and ordered a black coffee from the waiter whose cheeriness was the only respite in her bleak world.

'And what brings you to Miami? Spending Louis's money already?'

Miranda's head flew up to match the voice to the face. Catherine was the last person on earth she expected to see or wanted to see at this moment.

Catherine, as cool and elegant as ever, sat herself down at the white-clothed table across from Miranda and ordered herself a herbal tea and then, with a cool smile, gave Miranda her undivided attention.

'Can't say love suits you, dear, or does that explain your dull appearance—too much love? Louis always was very demanding.'

'So you keep telling me,' Miranda parried. Furious with herself for coming down in jeans and T-shirt and giving Catherine reason to comment, furious for allowing that comment about Louis to offend her so deeply.

'So what are you doing here? Louis didn't mention you yesterday so I presumed you were back on that dull island replenishing your shell collection.'

She'd seen him! Miranda's heart drummed miserably. He hadn't wasted much time. It hurt, badly.

'My uncle died last week,' Miranda told her, not expecting or getting a condolence.

'Funny, Louis didn't mention that either.' She smiled sweetly. 'Don't say you've had a lovers' tiff...?'

'We're not lovers, Catherine,' Miranda told her firmly, holding the other woman's cool blue eyes. 'We never were and we never will be. I was a business arrangement, as you well know.'

'Yes, of course, I was forgetting; but am I really expected to believe you weren't lovers? After what I went through on San Paola?' Her eyes narrowed and she leaned forward in her seat. 'Don't tell me he left you high and dry as well? I did warn you, Miranda, dear.'

There was no mistaking the satisfaction in her tone. She believed Louis had dropped her and Miranda wasn't about to expand on the painful truth.

'I'm surprised, though,' Catherine went on, confident now that Miranda was in the same boat as herself. 'When I left Miami to join him down there I was convinced I'd get him back. We'd been going through a bad patch in our affair, but it wasn't insurmountable—not till he picked you up from your little hide-out. I saw the change in him then, should have got out with my pride still in one piece.' She shrugged as if it didn't matter any more. 'He was besotted with you—a scruffy urchin—I could hardly believe what my eyes were telling me. He never took his from you. It was quite sickening.' She smiled warmly at Miranda. 'It didn't last, though, did it? Surprising, really; I thought it was the real thing for him this time. Never mind. It gives me a certain satisfaction to know that it didn't work out for you both. If you did but know it, dear, you did me an enormous favour. I've a new love in my life—someone who doesn't want to bury himself on some boring island in the Caribbean, miles from civilised society...'

Oh, Catherine, Miranda breathed happily inside. If you think I've done you a favour it's nothing to the enormous one you've bestowed on me. Confident now that Miranda was no longer a part of Louis's life, the blonde woman rambled on, but Miranda didn't hear. All she could think of was Louis on his island, Louis loving her, Louis besotted with her.

Why hadn't she seen it all before? Why hadn't she seen the looks he hadn't been able to hide from Catherine? Her uncle and his demanding agreement were gone now and Louis still wanted to marry her, but she hadn't wanted to believe it, too hurt and wrapped up in herself she hadn't seen what was in front of her face.

'Why are you crying, dear?'

'Crying?' Miranda sobbed; she hadn't realised she was, but oh, it was bliss to let the tears fall at last. She dabbed at her eyes with a napkin. 'I was thinking about my uncle—my clever, wicked, crooked uncle...'

'I don't understand,' Catherine murmured, the perplexities of that beyond her.

Miranda got to her feet. 'No, you wouldn't, Catherine.' She smiled through her tears. 'It was good to see you again. I hope everything goes well for your future.' She meant it, every sincere word.

'Likewise, I'm sure,' muttered Catherine as Miranda hurried away.

Miranda slammed the door of the suite shut and really cried then, left the floodgates wide open on her emotions and let it all out. She wept over the loss of her uncle, who, with the best intentions within his capabilities, had put her into the care of Louis, and she cried for Louis, inwardly begged for his forgiveness.

When her tears were spent, she washed her face and hurried to the phone. Catherine had seen him yesterday—how and where she didn't know or care. It was enough to know that he was still here in Miami.

'Did Louis Mendoza leave a forwarding address when he booked out of suite 503?' she asked the receptionist of the hotel, her fingers crossed that he hadn't already left for San Paola.

'He never left the hotel, Miss Gordon. He's in suite 504. Shall I connect you?'

'Please,' she cried. He hadn't left. He'd stayed, knowing that sooner or later she would come to her senses.

'Miranda?'

Miranda clutched the receiver joyfully. He'd answered the phone immediately, expecting her to call.

'How did you know it was me?' she murmured softly.

'I willed it.' She knew he was smiling, could hear it in his voice.

'I need to see you——' The line went dead before she could say any more.

Seconds later he was at the door and Miranda opened it, took both his hands and drew him into the room. He looked down at her, so tired, so weary with torn emotions that she knew he'd been going through the same hell as her.

'I love you, Louis,' she murmured through a smile, lifted her hands to stroke the side of his wonderful face. 'I love you, I want you, I need you. I want to go home, I want you to offer me a rainbow, for life.'

He smiled down at her, tilted her chin up with the tip of his finger. 'So many needs and wants; am I up to giving you all you ask?' he husked.

'Everything and more, my love, but first I need your forgiveness. I've been hateful to you—blind and stupid and childish. Catherine of all people made me see everything clearly...'

'Catherine?' His brow creased and Miranda smoothed it with the tips of her fingers.

'I was downstairs having a coffee and she joined me. She didn't realise what she was saying, she thought she was still abusing me and putting me down, but in fact she was telling me all the wonderful things that I hadn't realised for myself. I'm ashamed, Louis,' she said suddenly.

'Hey, no more of that,' he coaxed, sliding his arms around her waist.

'I mean it,' she said, leaning her head on his chest, hearing his heartbeat deep inside him. 'I thought the very worst of you, didn't believe that you loved me for myself. I was obsessed with this agreement between you and my uncle.'

'That's understandable.' He grazed his lips across her hot forehead. 'You've hardly been surrounded by love and warmth in your life. Presler let you down, and your uncle...'

Miranda lifted her head. 'I understand him now, Louis.'

'I always did, more so when I met you. He did some bad things in his life but he loved you, and it couldn't have been easy for him to bring you up. He had no love in his own life to guide him by. He thought he could buy your happiness for you; it was the only way he knew. In a way I'm glad he did—how else would we have met but for him and his crazy agreement?' His mouth came to hers, so soft and warm and loving that she felt tears of happiness fill her eyes. She let one slip and he drew away from her.

Louis smoothed it away with his thumb. 'I've been waiting for days for those,' he said.

'Tears?' she uttered.

'You were so uptight after your uncle died. You bottled your grief and your uncertainties inside you. That had to be released before you could come to me.'

'Is that why you stayed so close?'

He nodded and smiled. 'I know you, Miranda Gordon, better than you know yourself.'

She linked her arms around his neck. 'You didn't know I loved you, though. I've never told you before, have I?'

'I knew you did when I made love to you on the beach. You're not the type to let yourself go so completely if you aren't powered by love. Nor am I. I loved you so much I lost control.'

Miranda moved her hands down to his hips. 'Do you really love me?' she murmured suggestively.

'Yes, and I'm losing control again.' His lips sought hers, differently this time, impassioned and desperate, raising such heat and fire in her that her head spun. 'I want to marry you so desperately I'd give those islands to charity if it meant choosing between the two of you,' he grated, tearing his mouth from hers.

Miranda smiled through her tears of happiness. 'No choice, Louis. You have us both. I want to spend my life with you and our Operation Paradise, us and our children.'

'Children?' he echoed throatily. 'You're putting more ideas in my head.'

He lifted her up into his arms, carried her through to the bedroom and lay her down on the bed. Slowly he removed each article of her clothing, raining kisses on each part of her heated flesh he newly exposed. Miranda let her body and her mind float dizzily under his touch, murmuring her love with every breath that escaped from her lips. She touched and caressed too, eased his clothes from his magnificent body till they lay naked together, so close that not a whisper of air could pass between them.

'I want you forever, Miranda, my darling—you and I on our sunny island forever.'

'You have me, Louis.' She parted her lips for him as he bent over her, let her fingers trail over his body, touching him, arousing him till a mist of love and need enveloped them.

There was no discomfort now, no sand or rain to add to the fever and yet it rose as frantically as if it were the last time they would ever make love.

Louis drew hard on her inflamed nipples, drew back, half afraid of hurting her, but she arched her back insistently, wordlessly urging him to new depths of passion. He kissed and caressed every inch of her willing flesh and she loved and adored every part of him. Wanton in her exploration, uninhibited in the pleasure she wanted to give him. Her lips touched, mouthed her love, her tongue caressed every part of him till his breathing, inflamed and ragged, seemed to fill the room.

'Incredible,' he moaned as he lay on his back watching her adoration moving against him till his lips bared over his teeth and he could bear it no longer. He reached down for her and rolled her over and she parted her legs urgently, crying out with joy as he thrust into her. Rain and sun, their sweet love-moisture and their shining love mingled, coupled, forming the rainbow of their life. Higher and higher it rose in the sky of the future, arcing into the wild blue yonder and exploding into a myriad colours, and brightness and love. Together they rose and fell, together they would always rise and fall. The climax of their love was as eternal and as magical as the forming of a rainbow.

Next month's Romances

Each month, you can choose from a world of variety in romance with Mills & Boon. These are the new titles to look out for next month.

DISHONOURABLE PROPOSAL Jacqueline Baird

MISTAKEN ADVERSARY Penny Jordan

NOT HIS KIND OF WOMAN Roberta Leigh

GUILTY Anne Mather

DELIBERATE PROVOCATION Emma Richmond

DEAREST TRAITOR Patricia Wilson

ISLAND PARADISE Barbara McMahon

SUMMER'S ECHO Lee Stafford

MY ONLY LOVE Lee Wilkinson

RAINBOW OF LOVE Kay Gregory

CIRCLES OF DECEIT Catherine O'Connor

LOVE ISLAND Sally Heywood

THE INTRUDER Miriam Macgregor

A HEART SET FREE Nicola West

RENT-A-BRIDE LTD Emma Goldrick

STARSIGN

FORGOTTEN FIRE Joanna Mansell

Available from Boots, Martins, John Menzies, W.H. Smith, most supermarkets and other paperback stockists.

Also available from Mills & Boon Reader Service, P.O. Box 236, Thornton Road, Croydon, Surrey CR9 3RU.